Also by Lauran Paine
in Large Print:

The Apache Kid
The Devil on Horseback
The Manhunter
The Prairieton Raid
Timberline
Greed at Gold River
Moon Prairie
The Renegade
Thunder Valley
The Arizona Panhandle
The Open Range Men
Riders of the Trojan Horse
The Squaw Men
The Undertaker

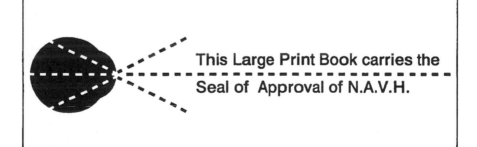

This Large Print Book carries the
Seal of Approval of N.A.V.H.

THE TRIANGLE MURDER

Lauran Paine

G.K. Hall & Co.
Thorndike, Maine

Published in 1996 by arrangement with
Robert Hale, Ltd., and Golden West Literary Agency.

G.K. Hall Large Print Paperback Collection.

The text of this Large Print edition is unabridged.
Other aspects of the book may vary from the original edition.

Set in 16 pt. Bookman Old Style by Rick Gundberg.

Printed in the United States on permanent paper.

Library of Congress Cataloging in Publication Data

Paine, Lauran.
    The triangle murder / by Lauran Paine.
        p.   cm.
    ISBN 0-7838-1898-X (lg. print : sc)
    1. Large type books. I. Title.
[PS3566.A34T75 1996]
813'.54—dc20   96-24307

THE TRIANGLE MURDER

CHAPTER 1

FOREST HILLS

Ordinary events seemed to flow through the tranquil atmosphere of fashionable Forest Hills in Southern California as though the world never had crises. Anything climactic or threatening stopped at the great stone pillars marking the entrance to Forest Hills. Beyond, where estates filled the gently rolling, green hills, was an orderly world that had been well lubricated by wealth for several generations.

It took a great deal of money to live beyond those stone markers, and the people who had lived there longest knew all the tricks, not just for making money, but all the little tricks for keeping it as well.

There were professional people, doctors, lawyers, accountants with extensive practices, a few motion picture people — although they were not popular in Forest Hill — and there were people like the Richard

Marchants, whose mercantile interests were nation-wide.

The entire atmosphere was restful. Horse paddocks behind handsome white wooden fences bordered small man-made lakes, and bridle trails that wound over and around the rolling countryside where immense oak trees lent a permanent kind of ageless shade in summertime to a semi-rural community whose sole existence for being was so that wealthy people could live in absolute comfort and seclusion, was what Forest Hills was all about.

Now and again outsiders caused a little trouble, but generally, because the police patrolled Forest Hills day and night, the serenity was undisturbed. It was so serene, in fact, and quiet, and proper, that Peter Marchant, the father of Richard, whose estate sat like a lord's manor house atop a wide, low hillock, once described Forest Hills as a place where birds came to make nests, where children grew up in absolute security, and where people came to waste their years being waited on, until they could die and get the hell out of Forest Hills.

But Peter Marchant was an old man, probably close to his seventies if not already into them, and he had come up by tooth and nail in an era when businessmen could not rely on government contracts to make them rich, but had to do it entirely by their own initiative and toughness. He was, in fact, something of an embarrassment to his son, Richard, and to his son's wife, Eleanor — who was one of the Whitings of Virginia. Old Dominion Virginia, in fact.

He did not live in the twenty-room fieldstone mansion atop the hill, either. He had insisted on having his own four-room house on the far end of the slope overlooking the stable and paddocks, the man-made lake, and the fields of the other estates. And to prove that he did not hold his son's way of life in great regard, he had had his cottage built facing away from the mansion, overlooking the distant hills in the direction of Los Angeles, which he could see on a clear day — of which there were few because of the polluted air.

Around Forest Hills people did not act quite patronisingly towards old Peter Marchant; after all, he was the founder of the immense Marchant fortune, something that mattered more in Forest Hills than anything else, but if it were possible to avoid the old man, people did it. He was too blunt, too opinionated, too earthy and plebeian for the cultivated taste of Forest Hills.

His son's wife suffered anguish each Saturday when the old man went down to the stable and helped Clyde Scruggs, the stableman, clean the corrals and stalls, and wash out the day-sheets and horse-blankets. She had complained any number of times to her husband. If any of their friends ever happened along while the old man was working like a common stableboy, she told Richard, she would cringe.

Richard, who resembled old Peter in his height and breadth, and his ruddy colouring and dark grey eyes, but who lacked the bear-trap mouth and the hard jaw, had simply said, "I've mentioned it to him, Eleanor. What else can I do?"

Eleanor's answer usually skirted close to what she wished Richard *would* do, but which she knew would make him angry if she ever said it: Get rid of the old man. Send him to a nice home for old people. At least find him an apartment in the city, regardless of the cost, and see that he was looked after. That was what Eleanor longed to say and never said, for a very good reason: if old Peter hadn't been able to instil in his only child the same strength of character Peter had, at least he *had* instilled in him some of the rough-hewn virtues, and one of those had to do with being loyal to one's family.

Old Peter would hike over the countryside, and that was another thing that mortified Eleanor Whiting Marchant. Her friends would recount, some with a droll slyness, that they had encountered her father-in-law hiking through their pastures, staff in hand, and although none said it, Eleanor understood their silent amusement because her father-in-law never dressed; he was always clean, but he was also always clad in old faded trousers and worn work-shirts.

Clarence Dunning, who owned a very lucrative investment banking business in Los Angeles, once told Lamont Blassingame, both of whose estates adjoined the Marchant estate, that while he rather liked old Peter Marchant, it did seem a pity the old gentleman wouldn't take some pride in himself, if not for his own satisfaction, then for Eleanor's and Richard's sake. Monty Blassingame's reply had been straightforward, which was the way Monty Blassingame always was.

"I think Eleanor and Richard have enough pride for the whole Marchant family. I like seeing the old man tramping the hills with his staff. It reminds me that some day, if I'm fortunate, I may have the health and the will to do the same thing."

But Monty Blassingame's opinion, if Eleanor had ever had it revealed to her, would not have counted for much. She had told Richard more than once that Lamont Blassingame might have the name and the wealth to qualify for residency in Forest Hills, but he talked and acted like someone's chauffeur.

As a matter of fact, Lamont Blassingame was acknowledgeably one of the two or three wealthiest residents of Forest Hills. He was a widower, and each spring and autumn when the local hunt club had a ball, although Lamont Blassingame did not belong, never rode, and had said more than once that the dumbest animal on earth was a horse, he was always invited, and he always attended — and he also swore up and down afterwards that he would never attend again.

The reason he was invited was no secret; everyone who belonged to the hunt club, and this included all but a small handful of local people, brought along either an unmarried cousin, a widowed sister, or perhaps a divorced close friend. One of the wealthiest men of Forest Hills who happened to also be unattached, was almost worth the trouble the women invariably went to, to make themselves irresistible. But Lamont Blassingame had a very high level of resistance to irresistible ladies, evidently, because seven years after the passing of his wife, he was still single.

He lived alone, with a couple, the woman looked after his mansion, the man looked after Monty Blassingame and the grounds, and seemed quite content to have it that way.

He spent a good bit of his time on the very elegant, raised rear patio behind his fifteen-room house where there was a magnificent view, and a swimming pool.

This patio, being raised so that in order to reach it one had to climb three long, wide stone steps, also had a quite ornate metal awning along the back of the house, as much to prevent late-day sunglare from reaching inside as to shade the half-dozen or so chaise-longues and chairs out there. It was at a round metal table well within the periphery of that delightful shade that Monty Blassingame usually sat in mid-morning and read his mail, the morning paper, the *Wall Street Journal*, and drank two cups of creamed and sweetened Bolivian coffee.

From that raised patio he had a magnificent view down across the rolling miles of Forest Hills. He could also be seen up there on the patio, providing a person happened to be looking. The shade obscured much of the back of the house, so it was improbable that someone riding past on the bridle path, which lay north of the house a quarter-mile or so, would see anyone on the patio unless they were expecting to see someone out there, or knew where to look.

Like most Forest Hills residents, Blassingame was jealous of his seclusion and his privacy. He did not welcome intrusions or uninvited guests, and because this was generally known, he was seldom annoyed by people dropping by. John Larkin, his combination chauffeur and yardman, once told the Marchants' stableman, Clyde Scruggs, that it was a pure pity that a man no older than Lamont Blassingame was, in his early fifties, should have been permitted to amass such an enormous fortune, because since the passing of his wife all he had been doing was take an infrequent swim, occasionally saddle one of the horses and ride a bit, spend one-half of almost every blessed morning out there on the patio, and eat and sleep.

There was, actually, a little more that Monty Blassingame did, but the objection of his man was valid enough, if, of course, one assumed that John Larkin had any right to pass a judgement upon the man he worked for, at least if he had any right to pass a judgement aloud, because eventually it got back to Eleanor and Richard, up at the big house, and became one of those cherished bits of juicy local information that people, rich or poor, delighted in storing away. It seemed not to matter where people congregated, in grubby little rural towns, in neighbourhood communities, or in very exclusive and serene estate localities such as Forest Hills, they still delighted in learning as much about the personal affairs of their neighbours as they could.

When Clyde Scruggs repeated Larkin's observation to old Peter Marchant, though, the reaction was different. "I learned when I was younger than you are, Clyde, that if a man just minded his own business he would have a full-time occupation. And who's to say Blassingame can't sit on his patio? It's his money, his estate, his damned patio."

Monty Blassingame never knew he had a defender; in fact, Monty Blassingame never even knew he'd had a detractor in his employee, John Larkin, because the morning of Wednesday, the second week of May, one of those most rare of all springtime days within several hundred miles of Los Angeles in any direction, when the sky was utterly clear and translucent in a pale and gorgeous way, John Larkin's wife went to take Lamont Blassingame his second cup of coffee, and reported back to her husband in the kitchen that poor Mister Blassingame had fallen sound asleep out there with his head on the table.

When Larkin went to see for himself a half-hour later, he noticed something his wife had quite fortunately overlooked — there was a spreading puddle of very dark red blood beneath the table Mister Lamont was sleeping on.

He wasn't sleeping, he was dead, and it wasn't a Forest Hills kind of death, either. Lamont Blassingame was dead from a bullet through the head.

CHAPTER 2

PAUL FLEMING'S
ASSIGNMENT

One of the things people said about Paul
Fleming was that as a detective he was
probably as good as any man connected
with the Los Angeles Police Department;
probably as good at his trade as any detective throughout the entire state of California, but they also said that his iconoclastic
character made him at times unnecessarily
rough in temperament and blunt in speech.

He was one of those men noted in every
profession whose dedication and impatience
made him at times the despair of the people
who had to work with him. And yet he was
very seldom irritable around people who
were willing but inexperienced. The people
he could wither with a glance were most
commonly those who were dense, or those
who talked down to him or who tried to
impress him.

It was said, not very long after his assignment to the Blassingame murder case, that if the Powers That Be in the Los Angeles Police Department had combed their five-thousand-man force for someone *un*suited to the job of winning friends for the L.A.P.D. in aristocratic Forest Hills, they could not possibly have found a better man.

But it happened that the Powers That Be were not elective officials, and therefore, as dedicated crimefighters, they were solely and exclusively interested in finding a murderer, and on that basis they could not have sent a better man out to Forest Hills.

It also happened that because Forest Hills was in the *county* of Los Angeles, not the *city*, Lamont Blassingame's murder had occurred outside the jurisdiction of the city police, in the territory of the county sheriff's office. But, as the undersheriff told Captain McLeod when he called in for help, Blassingame's murder was the kind of thing the sheriff's department was not really equipped to handle. So Paul Fleming had been sent down, on loan, as it were, but independent in fact of the sheriff's department, something the undersheriff had agreed to instantly, when Captain McLeod had told him who he would assign: Paul Fleming, the detective's detective, a man the sheriff's department had butted heads with on other occasions.

Fleming was a man of average height,

powerful in build, with sandy hair and the kind of bright blue eyes that were the mirrors to a bear-trap mind. He was at times taciturn, and at other times downright disagreeable, but he knew the law as well as any lawyer, and he knew detection better than nine-tenths of California's law-enforcement people. On top of these two things Fleming had one attribute that inevitably set him apart; he was highly intelligent in a dogged and tough-minded way.

Of course he knew where Forest Hills was, and he'd heard the usual rumours about its exclusiveness, and the kind of wealth, and therefore power, that was concentrated there. But as a matter of fact when he drove down to the Blassingame estate Thursday morning, one day after the corpse had been discovered and after it had been taken away, and also after all the L.A.P.D. laboratory people had gone over the place from top to bottom, from inside and outside, it was the first time Paul Fleming had ever seen Forest Hills.

He was impressed. In fact he wasted a full hour after passing through the entrance just cruising back and forth becoming oriented. By the time he went back to talk to John and Mary Larkin he knew who lived on each side of Blassingame, and a good deal more, and what he hadn't learned just from driving around, he made notes of so that when he returned to the city he could find out. No doubt a lot of it would be superfluous information, but Fleming was reconciled to that, too. He was a very thorough policeman, and he was also a career cop, so he could, and did, take his time. One of the advantages of being assigned to a murder case was that no sense of urgency impelled a man; the victim was not going anywhere; at least, he was not going anywhere *else*.

Fleming cruised up the winding road to the Blassingame residence taking down big sweeps of the fresh, clean, countryside air, and admiring the beautiful rolling fields, the white fences, the sleek horses that grazed the bluegrass paddocks, and when he got out of the car in front of the magnificent Blassingame residence he stood a long time leaning upon the car door just looking. Forest Hills had been laid out to be restful to the eyes, and it most certainly was. Particularly to a man who had grown almost to maturity in the country, and who had a strong streak of nostalgia in his make-up.

Then Paul Fleming went up to the house, as brisk and professional as he usually was, and knocked on the door. An hour later he had finished talking to the Larkins, an interlude that proved hardly worth the effort, except that routine required it. They knew nothing of their employer's personal affairs. They had been with Lamont Blassingame six years, and during that time, between the grounds and the house, and their own singular lack of interest in things that were none of their business, they had worked hard, banked their pay, and kept pretty much to themselves.

They were people in their late thirties, both of them, usually circumspect, and quite content to be away from the city, things that Paul Fleming had already deduced because otherwise they never would have stayed in secluded and semi-rural Forest Hills for six years, a place where retainers could enjoy the scenery, good pay, and little else, thanks to a pronounced caste system.

Fleming prowled the house, and although he had no warrant to allow it, he also prowled the beautifully furnished, rosewood-panelled study, and the equally as magnificent, and very large and old, desk. He needed two things, right at the moment, and the desk supplied one of them, a lawyer's name. When Fleming sat back, lit a cigarette and savoured, for a little while, the luxury of being in Lamont Blassingame's home, chair, and exalted position, he thought that the Blassingame murder case was going to be one of those easily resolved situations motivated by greed and nothing else. They were the simplest of all murders to investigate.

Then he talked to the lawyer, Eric

Frederickson of Frederickson, Martin & Bishop, and got his first chilly premonition. There was, indeed, an heir, a woman named Elisabeth Maitland who was a missionary in Thailand. She had been in Thailand four years. She was Lamont Blassingame's only relative, by his own account, and according to Eric Frederickson, Blassingame had willed his entire estate to her.

That supplied the second thing Fleming had needed; the name, relationship, and probable association between the murdered man and his heir. Fleming put down the telephone for a moment, then raised it and dialled Michael Sublette, his occasional associate in homicide assignments.

"I need everything you can dig up on a woman named Elisabeth Maitland," Fleming said. "She's a missionary in Thailand, niece to Lamont Blassingame, his only heir — and he's been hauled away with a bullet in his head."

Sublette said, "All right, I'll get right on it. Tell me, Paul — couldn't you have found an heir in Tibet?"

Fleming allowed himself a flicker of a smile as he put aside the telephone, put out his cigarette in a sterling ashtray with a fluted Venetian glass dish moulded to the silver, then dialled another number and rocked back again in the large leather swivel-chair. This time he spoke to an assistant coroner.

The bullet that had killed Lamont Blassingame was from a .30-.06 rifle, probably the most common sporting rifle in the United States, one that had been around since before Fleming had been born. Thirty-ought-six barrels, and even the entire weapon, modernised and sporterised, had been mass-produced during the First World War, and although superseded many times over for military use since, remained as the least expensive, most common and most numerous rifle for hunters.

The assistant coroner had the bullet and would send it along to L.A.P.D. ballistics where, no doubt, it would be categorised as to its individuality, but of course unless the rifle from which the slug had been fired were found, the bullet by itself would be practically useless. Fleming rang off thinking that by now the rifle, which had probably been bought for peanuts, had been flung into the sea, buried six feet deep in the earth, or perhaps even melted down and discarded as ash.

He sat a long while in the study. So long, in fact, that Larkin came diffidently to satisfy his curiosity, and masked this — he thought, by asking if Mister Fleming would like a spot of tea.

Fleming did not want any tea. He did not like tea, and since Larkin offered no coffee before slipping unobtrusively towards the back of the house again, Fleming went without, something that did not trouble him.

He telephoned the sheriff's department to speak to the officer who had first answered the call from the Blassingame residence. When he had him on the line Fleming asked about the wound.

The deputy said, "Assuming he was facing the direction he was sitting in the chair at the table — which would be west and slightly south — I'd say that the bullet hit him just in front of the ear on the right side on a slightly upward angle, fired from a northerly direction."

Fleming said, "Thanks," put down the telephone, finally got up out of the luxurious leather chair and ambled out back to the raised patio where the shade, along with flower-fragrance, should have had a drowsing, soporific effect.

If the bullet struck Blassingame in the head on the right side, it had been fired from northward. The fact that it had taken off the top of his head or, as the deputy had said, had struck him on an angle, did not have to mean the murderer was kneeling or even crouching, because the patio was several feet higher than the surrounding terrain, and a marksman standing perfectly erect firing at someone seated up there on the patio would have been slightly elevated. Particularly so since the land sloped away, downward in all directions from the Blassingame mansion.

Northward was the tree-shaded bridle trail, otherwise there was one of those white-painted pasture fences on both sides of the trail, beyond which was more gently rolling, green countryside with an occasional mighty oak tree. Unless the murderer had stood out in the middle of one of the large paddocks, in plain sight, and fired, and assuming he would instinctively seek protective cover rather than be all that exposed, why then he must have fired from down by the bridle path.

Fleming struck out from the patio across a warm, grassy pasture, climbed two white fences, and eventually reached the trail, which was about fifteen feet wide, fenced on both sides, blessedly shaded, and delightfully peaceful. There, he turned and looked back.

Blassingame's residence stood out like a medieval manor house, its broad eaves protecting half the stone-and-wood walls, shading the sparkling windows, and along the rear where the patio was, the extended overhang provided a very broad expanse of shade.

Fleming could see the table where Blassingame's body had fallen forward. He could also see most of the patio furniture, but the longer he stood and looked, the more it seemed highly unlikely that, unless the marksman had known exactly where to look, and *for whom* to look, he would have known someone was sitting up there deep in the shade.

Larkin had mentioned that occasionally pheasant and quail hunters tramped through the countryside, and Fleming had discarded that at once on the grounds that pheasant and quail hunters did *not* use rifles, they used shotguns.

Larkin had also mentioned an occasional youth with a small-calibre rifle, perhaps a .22, being out after rabbits, but again, there was hardly any comparison between a .22-calibre slug and a .30-.06 bullet.

What baffled Fleming was that neither of the Larkins had heard the shot; a thirty-ought-six had a muzzle blast that could be heard, in a quiet place like Forest Hills, for up to a mile. Closer than that, there was no way *not* to hear it, assuming the Larkins had just average hearing.

Fleming lit a cigarette, loosened his tie and slouched beside a monarch black oak tree. Above him some birds protested his presence bitterly. He did not even glance up.

Aside from the fact that the Larkins hadn't heard a gunshot, and aside from the fact that Fleming's preconceived notion of this being a murder for money, there was one other thing that troubled him. According to the Larkins, their employer was almost a recluse; he certainly was not exceptionally gregarious, and although he occasionally went to parties, he did not as a general rule associate very much with his neighbours and local acquaintances — so, it was very unlikely he had been shot by a jealous husband or an outraged wife.

Then why the hell *had* he been shot? A crime without a motive was about as amenable to understanding as was a man in his prime, with all the money he would ever need, being content to sit on a patio reading the *Wall Street Journal*.

CHAPTER 3

A TIME WITHOUT LEADS

Because it was customary to start *some-where*, Paul Fleming clung to the matter of the muzzle blast. He knew both John and Mary Larkin had average or better hearing because while he had interviewed them in the spacious sitting-room of the Blassin-game mansion, despite the fact that he had spoken in his usual quiet tone of voice, neither of them had experienced the slight-est difficulty hearing what he had said.

Both had been in the house when their employer had been killed, so they *should* have heard the gunshot. The fact that they were both adamant on this score inclined Fleming to discount them as suspects be-cause, unless they were a lot more dense than Fleming thought they were, they most certainly would have realised that by saying they had not heard the shot, when they were the only people at the scene of the murder, placed them in an awkward position.

Fleming walked a short distance down the bridlepath scuffing earth, then he reversed himself and did the same thing walking up the trail, but there was no .30-.06 brass cartridge case. He had not really expected to find one. The kind of weapon he was certain had been used had to be manually manipulated to eject the spent casing. The murderer — anyone at all who could shoot a man in the head in poor light from that distance — was thoroughly familiar with his weapon, and would be calm enough not to eject a shell casing. But, as with the routine interrogation of the Larkins, this was the kind of thing a detective was supposed to do. Sometimes it paid off, most of the time it did not. But in the game of manhunting the rules were fairly well prescribed and Paul Fleming, the old hand, went through the ritual every time.

He also stood in the tranquility of a bright sunshiny morning with birdsong all around, studying the countryside. If a killer had come up this far along the bridle path, he had probably been seen. If he came on foot he would have attracted some interest, and if he had been one of the local people and had come on horseback, he would still have been seen, because even if he had concealed the rifle some way, perhaps in a wrapping, that too would have looked unusual.

He went almost a mile in both directions

looking for footprints, and finding none he decided that the murderer had come on horseback. If that were so, then more than likely the person Fleming sought was a resident of Forest Hills, because the bridle trail was clearly posted against trespassers, meaning non-resident outsiders.

But before he got too involved with the local people he decided to go visit Eric Frederickson of the law offices of Frederickson, Martin & Bishop, and that was not just a long, hot drive, but the unhealthy air of the city, when he got back there, made an unpleasant contrast.

Frederickson was younger than Paul Fleming had expected. In fact, he seemed barely old enough to have graduated from law school, but as soon as Fleming was taken into his sumptuous private office and saw the portrait of the look-alike older man on a wall between two bookshelves, he understood that *this* Frederickson was not *the* Frederickson; was instead probably a son.

What Fleming wanted could not have been a mystery to Eric Frederickson. Fleming had barely sat down when the younger man said, "I sent off an airmail letter this morning to Miss Maitland, Inspector. If she complies with my request, she should be arriving here by the middle of next week. As for Mister Blassingame's personal affairs, you'll realise there isn't very much I can do, unless you get a court order."

Fleming sat and gazed at young Frederickson and wondered whether he was acting this way because he did not understand that, while his implication was correct, most law offices cooperated with the police, or whether he was just being contrary because he had an exalted opinion of himself.

Fleming said, "I'll get the order, but what I'd like right now is a couple of simple answers from you. One concerns Lamont Blassingame's personal life, one concerns his professional life, and neither, I think, will compel you to jeopardise the client-lawyer relationship."

Young Frederickson, a man with pale, downy cheeks and pale, light-blue eyes, a rather narrow face, and a receding hairline, smiled as he said, "I'll do what I can, of course," in an indulgent voice, and Fleming mocked him.

"Of course." Then Fleming asked his questions. "About Blassingame's personal life: who would his enemies be?"

Frederickson leaned on his desk, still looking indulgent. "I couldn't say. The firm's association with Mister Blassingame was never personal, always professional."

Fleming had thought some such answer would be forthcoming. "Fine. Then who would his professional enemies be?"

Frederickson sat a long moment gazing at

Paul Fleming. Finally he leaned back and said, "You are deceptive in appearance, Inspector."

Fleming kept smiling. He was not an inspector, he was a detective sergeant, and if he was deceptive it was only because young Frederickson saw him that way. Fortunately, regulations prohibited Fleming from telling young Frederickson what he looked like to Paul Fleming.

The attorney finally said, "Well, as a matter of fact, Mister Blassingame was semi-retired. He inherited a good bit of his wealth, and although he added to it over the years — in speculation stocks and bonds, real estate, so-forth — he was never an aggressive businessman, so how he could have made enemies is quite beyond me." Young Frederickson raised his eyebrows. "Inspector, isn't it feasible that the murderer was just some psychopathic leftist; some individual of diminished intellectual capacity who hated rich men?"

Fleming nodded. "It's possible," he conceded. "But if it's true, then I'm interested in why he picked Blassingame and not someone else; someone, for example, who lived closer to the outskirts of Forest Hills and therefore closer to the county roads."

Frederickson stared. "What can the county roads have to do with it, Inspector?"

"The killer had to go up that bridle path

over a mile to be close enough to the Blassingame residence to make his kill. There are a number of very rich men who live closer to the boundary of Forest Hills, Counsellor. If all he wanted to do was hit a rich man, why take all that unnecessary risk?"

Frederickson spread his hands. "Aren't you possibly attributing to an idiot more reasoning capacity than he probably had?"

Fleming gazed at the younger man. "All right. Maybe I am. So let's put it on a more physical plane. Why the hell would someone out to make a random killing walk over a mile on a hot day to shoot someone he didn't know, when he could have done the same thing, without any of the physical inconveniences, by shooting someone closer to the place where he probably entered Forest Hills? If he's just a mental vegetable, he would be even more conscious of physical discomfort, wouldn't he?"

The lawyer studied Fleming again, then said, "You *are* a deceptive individual, Inspector."

Fleming arose, angry but smiling. "If that's a compliment," he said, looking the lawyer squarely in the eye, "I wish I could return it. Now, suppose we get back to Blassingame's enemies."

Frederickson turned a pale shade of red. He and Paul Fleming were obviously flint on steel. But young Frederickson was polished;

he was not going to spring to his feet, insulted and angry. But he sat a long time before speaking again.

Eventually, without looking at Fleming, he said, "I cannot honestly think of a single soul who would want Lamont Blassingame dead. His niece alone will benefit. She certainly did not kill Mister Blassingame."

Fleming said, "Do you know her; have you ever met Miss Maitland?"

Frederickson shook his head. "No. I think she was in the States about five years ago. I seem to recall Mister Blassingame saying something like that, but he rarely mentioned her and I never asked. I had no need to. She was his heir, and until he passed on this office would have no real interest in her."

Fleming got out of there. Even the polluted air of the hot, sticky city was preferable to the rarified, snobbish air that came through the conditioners in the law offices of Frederickson, Martin & Bishop.

He drove to the Central Division and rode a lift to Mike Sublette's office. The air-conditioned atmosphere on the fourth floor of this building was cool, too, but it smelled of stale cigars, an aroma Fleming had long since become accustomed to.

Sublette was a large, rather thickly massive man with dark brown eyes and very dark curly hair. He looked more like some kind of Levantine rug merchant than a very skilled and knowledgeable detective. Also, being thick and almost square, although he dressed well he never quite *looked* presentable, particularly in hot weather when his clothing hung on him like sackcloth. The moment Paul Fleming entered, Sublette dived into a pile of untidy papers atop his desk and neglected to even offer a greeting until he came up with a yellow length of lined tablet paper. Then he said, "Glad to see you. Have a chair," and as soon as Fleming sat down Sublette said, "Elisabeth Maitland is a single woman, thirty-one years of age, has been a professional nurse for eight years, has a strong streak of Christian compassion in her and for six of those eight years has been serving missionary hospitals in weird places in Asia." Mike Sublette handed over the yellow piece of lined tablet paper. "A couple hundred years ago, from my deductions, she'd have entered a convent and gone slithering around dressed in black doing good works and scaring hell out of little kids . . . Is this your murder suspect? Because if it is, brother, you'd better go fall on your sword."

Paul Fleming lit a cigarette, pocketed the paper and smiled. "My man was hit by *someone*," he said.

"Not her," exclaimed Sublette, pointing towards the pocket Fleming had put the piece of lined paper into. "I verified through her

34

church affiliate, the hospital association, that the farthest she's gone from her junglerot compound in four years was once to Hong Kong, and that was two years ago. Otherwise, she's been right there putting poultices on yaws and exorcising evil spirits from rice-farmers in the form of belly worms for four years." Sublette yanked at his collar. He was one of those bull-necked individuals for whom neither shirtcollars nor ties had been made, nor ever seemed to fit. "Is she Blassingame's heir?"

Fleming nodded. "The only heir, in fact."

"How much will she get?"

Fleming had no idea, but he made a rough guess. "More by accident than you and I together could make in several lifetimes. Millions, I suppose."

That sobered Sublette. "Then she had the best motive under the sun. But she didn't shoot this guy from Thailand."

Fleming flicked ash. "How about a hired job?"

Sublette sighed. "I wouldn't guess. Not until I'd seen her and talked to her. Shouldn't you notify her?"

"The lawyer's already done that. By the way, did you ever talk to a lawyer you'd like to take across your knee?"

Sublette said, "Hell, no. But I've talked to dozens of them I'd like to feed a knuckle sandwich to."

Fleming doused his cigarette and arose. "Are you on an assignment right now, by any chance?"

Sublette wasn't. "Just wound one up yesterday afternoon. Why? Do you need help?"

"Maybe later," conceded Fleming. "Not right now. But hang loose if you can, Mike."

Sublette dismissed that request in three words. "Talk to McLeod."

Fleming went downstairs to Records and Files, spent the balance of the day looking up people with names like Larkin, John and Mary; Marchant, Richard and Eleanor; Scruggs, Clyde, and about a dozen other residents of Forest Hills. What he finished up with at the end of the day was four traffic violations and one citizen's arrest made by Clarence Dunning who lived on an estate south of the Blassingame place. Dunning had caught a trespasser red-handed prowling around his stable.

He took all the notes he had made on these things home with him to his apartment out in Westwood, along with the work-sheet Mike Sublette had got up on the Maitland woman, had a bottle of ale on his tiny terrace and conceded, as twilight settled, that he had probably the least promising alignment of suspects any homicide detective had ever come up with.

The beer at least was helpful.

CHAPTER 4

SOME RANDOM CONSIDERATIONS

Fleming had a long talk with the coroner's office the following day, from Lamont Blassingame's wonderfully restful study, and what he was told about the nature of the fatal wound drove him to call the ballistics people at Central Division in Los Angeles because it opened up a possibility that could, perhaps, answer one of the riddles.

In response to his question, the technician he spoke to said, "Yes, it's possible that the murder rifle was fitted with a silencer, but you've got to understand, Sergeant, that silencering a rifle is a hell of a lot different from silencering a revolver. For one thing, the silencer has to be made a lot better — stronger, longer, with better baffles inside — and for another thing it would absolutely detract from the rifle's range because it would inhibit muzzle velocity."

Fleming sighed to himself. He wasn't interested in the same things that interested the technician. He was not a gun buff, he was a homicide detective. "Can you tell from the slug sent over from the coroner's department, the one used to kill Lamont Blassingame, if the rifle was actually equipped with a silencer?"

The technician said, "Hold on a moment. I haven't looked at that particular report. Just hold on a moment."

Fleming sat back, lit a smoke, eyed the rows of books, the fluted beams of the ceiling, the terribly expensive rosewood furnishings, and by the time the ballistics expert returned he had decided that his next move would be to remorselessly rummage Blassingame's desk — without the necessary warrant.

"It *was* fitted with a silencer," said the technician, and Fleming thanked him, put the telephone down very gently, and leaned on the desk, staring out the doorway into the vacant hall.

Eventually, he strolled back to the patio, sat down in the same chair Blassingame had been sitting in when he'd been killed, and rested an arm upon the table. He had an unimpeded view of the northward bridle trail. There were the trees, of course, but otherwise he could see a long distance in both directions. Then he turned and gazed towards the west, and slightly to the south, which was probably the direction Blassingame had been facing when the bullet had struck him. There was nothing out there except rolling countryside and, through a screen of distant tall poplars, a large, low Moorish-type residence perhaps a half-mile or three-quarters of a mile away.

Blassingame, Paul Fleming was quite certain, had not been the victim of some killcrazy individual. And whoever had killed him had known his habits, and had also known the best place to stand and take aim when they killed him. John Larkin would be a very nice suspect, except that Larkin was one of those thick-hided, somewhat phlegmatic people for whom even insults had no very great and lasting significance. Also, both the Larkins had stated quite emphatically that Lamont Blassingame was the best man they had ever worked for, very kindly and very lenient.

Fleming arose with a groan. *Someone* hadn't viewed him in that light. He went down towards the stable and stood in hot shade down there thinking back a good many years when the kind of smell that was around him had been familiar, had in some indefinable way meant security to a country boy.

He looked at the horses, at the saddles and bridles and strolled out back where the hayshed stood. None of this had anything to do with solving a murder, but for a little while he didn't care.

He was still down there when Larkin came along to pitch out some feed. Larkin was a large-boned, complacent individual, the kind who could have been double-barrelled trouble if he'd had a mean streak, because he was large and rangy and strong. But John Larkin was a pleasant, quiet-spoken man, not the kind to ever win many laurels, but the kind of a man someone like Lamont Blassingame would have appreciated.

Fleming leaned on a rack and watched the older man do his chores. He said, "To set your mind at rest, Mister Larkin, in case you were worrying, the lawyers for the estate have notified Mister Blassingame's heir."

Larkin looked around, his weathered, calm face showing friendliness. "I know. We got a telegram this afternoon from Miss Maitland. She wants me and the missus to stay on until she gets here."

Fleming nodded, then he said, "When was the last time Mister Blassingame had business associates to the estate?"

Larkin answered calmly, the way he always answered questions. "Never, that I know of, Sergeant Fleming. He hardly ever had folks in. When he did, they might be the Marchants or someone like that."

Fleming left, ambling back over towards the bridle path, and behind him Larkin

40

leaned pensively upon a pitchfork and watched him walk away.

It seemed to be getting hotter by the day, and it also seemed to be staying hotter. At the bridle path there was shade, but even standing in shade it was hot. Fleming had never seen any riders on the path, but today he saw two, a pair of young girls, perhaps in their early teens. They stared long and un- abashedly at Fleming, leaning against an oak tree chewing a stalk of grass, watching them. When they came abreast of him he smiled because they seemed about to whirl and dash back the way they had come.

He understood their thoughts; by now everyone throughout Forest Hills knew about the Blassingame murder. Perhaps the young girls had decided to ride up this way just so that they could stare at a house where a genuine murder had taken place, and that would be scary enough, but to suddenly find a strange man standing near where the murderer had probably also stood would be just about the limit the courage of young girls would extend.

When he was certain they were about to whirl and bolt, Fleming said, "Those are sure beautiful horses." They weren't, actually; both were mares and both were too fat and dumpy.

The girls stared and nodded and offered a couple of wavery smiles. They kept on riding, got past, and a dozen yards onward whipped up their mounts and went bobbing up and down along the trail. Fleming laughed, leaned to watch, and when a man's gruff voice said, "You probably stunted their growth," Fleming turned and found himself face to face with a nut-brown old man who was walking up the bridle trail with a tall staff. Except for two things, the old man could have been someone's hired stable-hand. One thing was the Masonic ring with the Thirty-second Degree emblem and the perfect, large diamond set in the middle of the ring, and the other thing was the expression of total equality and head-high challenge the older man offered.

His shirt was an old, faded blue shirt, the kind stablemen might wear, and his trousers were cotton khaki, washables, the kind an old man might wear who had no wife to insist that he make a better appearance.

Fleming took it all in with a smile and one piercing look. As the old man paused and leaned on his staff he returned Fleming's scrutiny, then he said, "Detective, aren't you?" And Fleming fished for his packet of smokes as he answered.

"Yeah. Detective. Care for a cigarette?"

The old man shook his head. "Certainly not," but he said nothing else when Fleming lit up, and their eyes met and held.

"Peter Marchant," said the old man, by way

of self-introduction. He jutted with his chin towards a magnificent house atop a distant, fat hillock. "I live over there. Not in *that* house. Out back in a cottage." With this out of the way the old man returned to studying Paul Fleming. "Not making much headway, are you?"

Fleming had made his assessment. Old Peter Marchant was not the total stranger he might have assumed that he was. Fleming was thorough in his homework and in his research. He considered the tough old face and the stone-steady eyes, and said, "No headway at all, Mister Marchant." He turned to see where the little girls had got to, and Marchant snapped at him.

"When you're speaking to someone, don't turn away, look right at them."

Fleming turned back, not entirely surprised, but caught unprepared. The jaw, the thin lips, the hard, tough old eyes, had already told him the kind of a man old Peter Marchant had once been, and evidently still was.

Marchant said, "The shot came right from along here somewhere, didn't it?"

Fleming nodded. There were always people with nothing but curiosity in their favour who cluttered up homicide investigations, and sometimes there were men like Peter Marchant who were more interested than curious, and whose incisive minds made the difference. Fleming smoked and studied the old man, and waited.

Marchant finally said, "I'm seventy-one years old, and I've learned a few things about people you don't learn until you get that old. One of them is that no one does anything without a purpose. Another thing is that eight times out of ten the purpose isn't something they are proud of."

Fleming considered this, and slowly came to the conclusion that he liked the sound of it, so he said, "I think you're probably right. In Blassingame's case there is also the matter of punishment."

Peter Marchant's grey eyes went fleetingly towards the distant patio, then drifted back and settled upon Paul Fleming. "In Blassingame's case the purpose had to be a whole lot stronger than in most cases of human motivation. People who grow up believing it's wrong to kill people, even though they then go right ahead and do it, have to be driven by a very strong purpose."

Fleming exhaled smoke, returned the old man's stare, and finally said, "What's on your mind, Mister Marchant?"

The answer came back, as flat and hard as a ricocheting bullet. "You're the detective, young man." He took a fresh grip on his staff and turned away, crossed to the far fence, clambered over it and went stalking down across a big stretch of meadowland without once looking back.

Fleming dropped the cigarette, stamped on it, then leaned and watched until the old man was small in the heat-hazed distance where he began stalking up a slope towards the distant mansion, but on an angle that would carry him well away from it.

Fleming sighed. Sometimes the belief in law and order was enough to intimidate people; when a detective showed his badge and I.D. folder, reluctance to become involved dissolved. Not here in Forest Hills. These were a quite different variety of people. If they had a fear of anything it perhaps was the leftist drift, but it was not the law.

Fleming climbed back into the Blassingame paddock and strolled thoughtfully back towards the house. He was satisfied on two counts; one was that there was little more to be learned by haunting the Blassingame residence, and the second thing was that somewhere in Forest Hills there was someone who was not necessarily involved, but who certainly knew more than Fleming knew.

He stopped near the swimming pool and turned to look back where the old man had disappeared over the low, rolling hill, and the longer he stood looking back the more he wondered what would fill the life of an old man who had nothing, really, to do with his time but hike the countryside — or perhaps stand atop his hill with a pair of binoculars.

From over there to the bridle path was not a very great distance; with seven-by-thirty fieldglasses a man could, on a clear day, be able to see everything except up where Lamont Blassingame had been seated in the shade, quite well. Well enough, in fact, if he happened to be looking, to see sunshine reflect off a rifle barrel. In fact, for that a man wouldn't even need fieldglasses, but if he saw such a reflection, and if he lived close by, it wouldn't take him long to step to his house and return with the fieldglasses.

Fleming continued on around the Blassingame mansion to his car, without going back to the house to tell the Larkins he was leaving.

He drove back to the city in no great haste, and by the time he got there it was too late for Mike Sublette to still be in his office, but Fleming didn't particularly want to see Mike anyway. He went along to Captain McLeod's office, sat a while with the Chief of Detectives, and when he finally departed, homeward bound, he had McLeod's promise to assign Sublette to the Blassingame case.

The following day he did not return to Forest Hills. He and Mike Sublette had a quiet conference in the coffee shop across the street from Central Division Headquarters, and later on Paul Fleming ambled off to do some research on the Richard Marchants — and Peter Marchant — while Sublette undertook the quiet investigation of, among others, Lamont Blassingame's other neighbour, Clarence Dunning.

But the second day Fleming returned to Forest Hills, and his return was deliberately timed to coincide with the arrival of Saturday, when he knew the Marchants and Clarence Dunning would not be in the city.

CHAPTER 5

RENEWING AN ACQUAINTANCESHIP

Motive was always very important, but Paul Fleming never let its absence deter him because he liked something else just as well. Association. If there was no visible motive, or, as in the Blassingame case, it was tardy showing up, Fleming went after the other thing, and almost invariably the motive turned up all by itself.

But Lamont Blassingame, being a deliberately reticent person, almost, in fact, an anti-social person, it was almost as difficult finding his associates as it was finding someone's motive for murdering him. As Mike Sublette said over the telephone on Saturday morning before Fleming had left his apartment, "When a guy works in a factory or an office, he eats lunch with other people, shares business interests with them, and always has some fairly close friends. What can you do with a person worth several million dollars who doesn't seem to really care too much for people and stays away from them when he can?"

Fleming's reply had been short. "You dig, and claw, and dig some more, and eventually you come up with *something*."

When Sublette had called Fleming hadn't had breakfast. Later, on his way to Forest Hills he *had* had breakfast, and as any anthropologist or social scientist could have explained, regardless of the genus, male animals functioned best after being fed, especially in the early morning.

By the time Fleming wheeled up the Marchants' private road he was in a much better mood, and even the closed-face look he got from the servant who admitted him to the Marchant mansion could not dent his amiability. Even when Richard Marchant came out to the entry hall to shake his hand and gaze at him with an almost identical expression as he invited Sergeant Fleming into the main reception-room, Fleming's good nature would not be ruffled.

Marchant was a well-proportioned man, six feet tall, Fleming guessed, and about a hundred and eighty pounds. He had his father's grey eyes, but the lower part of his face showed a definite softness. Well, there really was no need for the son to be like the father. The old man had accumulated it, which was always the hardest part, and the son, surrounded by comfort and security, had only to learn how to hold on to it, and that did not require the same corsair-character at all.

Richard Marchant was pleasant, but Fleming kept getting vibrations of remoteness from him. It was not exactly an unusual attitude for people to take towards detectives. Particularly among people to whom any kind of notoriety was absolute anathema.

Fleming said, "Just a few questions about Lamont Blassingame, if you have the time."

Marchant motioned towards a beautiful red leather chair. "Of course, Sergeant. Please be seated."

Fleming sat. It was a lovely room, bright and airy, colourful, beautifully and very expensively furnished. Eleanor's touch was throughout. Fleming would get to her later. He already knew what she looked like and what he thought her personality would be like. He said, "I'm particularly interested in the association between the Marchants and Lamont Blassingame."

Richard Marchant accepted this without difficulty. "Neighbours," he replied. "Friends, too, but only socially. Monty was pleasant at parties." Marchant smiled slightly. "Sometimes he was a bit blunt. But that was Monty, and no one really thought much about it. He had very definite ideas about things."

"Antagonistic?" asked Fleming, and Marchant shook his head.

"Not really. At times he'd irritate a person, but, as I just said, that was Monty and most of us understood it."

"When he antagonised people, Mister Marchant —" Before Fleming got round to phrasing the question, Richard Marchant was already answering it.

"No, no, Sergeant. Not at all. After all, there'd be no reason to shoot him for something as trivial as being momentarily upset by something he said." Marchant offered that vague little indulgent smile again. "The people who live around here aren't susceptible, Sergeant. Not at that level."

"How about the hired help?" asked Fleming, wondering whether he dared light a cigarette, and deciding not to because he could detect no smoke-scent in the room.

Richard Marchant slowly shook his head. "I certainly would doubt that, Sergeant. Monty Blassingame didn't really have that much to do with any hired help but his own — the Larkins." Marchant paused, studying Fleming, then he said, "I suppose you can guess that among the neighbours they look like the logical suspects."

Fleming made his perfunctory, professional smile. "I can guess," he murmured, and watched the handsome man across from him. "How about other people's wives, Mister Marchant?"

That came a bit suddenly and Marchant blinked. "Other people's wives . . . ? Sergeant, Monty Blassingame was certainly not what you'd call a Casanova, neither by personality nor, as far as I know, by inclination." Marchant recovered, and even smiled. "He didn't even like to dance."

Fleming was not of the opinion that dancing was what motivated Casanovas, but he did not pursue this any further. "By any chance do you know anyone who was in any way associated with Blassingame in a business sense; maybe not *strictly* in the business sense, Mister Marchant? Perhaps someone who owed him money, or someone he might have financed. Anything like that."

Richard Marchant sat a moment in calm reflection, then slowly shook his head. "I really know very little about Monty's private affairs, Sergeant. Out here, we more or less live as independently as we can from business; from the things that make us drive into the city."

Fleming could appreciate that. What was the sense of residing in paradise if you had to bring the smell of sweat and anxiety and ulcer medicine home with you?

Fleming arose. "You have a wonderful view up here, Mister Marchant. Would you object to my walking out back and looking over the countryside?"

Richard Marchant arose, wearing a quizzical expression. He answered slowly. "No, I wouldn't object at all." Marchant, too, had made an assessment. It seemed to incline him towards a conviction that Sergeant Fleming was not the kind of a man who simply stood on hilltops admiring beautiful views because he possessed a lyrical soul.

When Fleming got back outside in the morning sunshine he paused once on his trip round the south side of the house to admire a particularly beautiful rose. He knew its name: Tropicana. Otherwise, he was not entirely oblivious to a sensation of being watched. That was neither a new nor even a unique sensation in Fleming's trade. He had the feeling even when he *wasn't* being watched, sometimes.

He had originally intended to also speak to Eleanor Whiting Marchant, but after the question about Blassingame's possible interest in other men's wives, Fleming decided to let his talk with Eleanor slide. At least for a day or two.

Out back, the landscaped grounds sloped slightly towards the west. Actually, they sloped away from the manor house in all directions, but Fleming was only concerned with their gradual slope towards the distant, immaculate and white-painted horse barn, and, to the south of that, mid-way between the stable area and the main residence, the delightful small cottage which would be where Peter Marchant resided.

By turning slightly towards the south Fleming could look down across the rolling meadow towards the white-fenced bridle trail, and on across into the oak-studded paddocks of the Blassingame estate. It was a beautiful and restful view. It was also a clear and revealing view.

It was not possible to see the rear of the Blassingame house from where Fleming stood, only the distant north side of the house. He strolled down closer to the little cottage, but it was still not possible to see the shaded patio out back of the Blassingame residence, except for one corner of it when he was almost to the cottage. But it was possible to see the bridle path for a fair distance south-west and north-east, where it came up from round a shaded low hill in the distance and meandered past the Blassingame place and on up towards the north-east. Whoever had laid out that path had had a good eye for natural blandishments. The trail was almost entirely shaded in several places, and even where riders had to cross out of oak-shade into bright sunlight they did not have to go far before reaching shade again.

It was a decidedly tranquil setting,

Fleming thought. It was also possible that he had been wrong about Blassingame's killer having to approach on horseback; there were enough trees to shield him quite handily, if he'd had in mind making a surreptitious or discreet approach, and even if riders had come along — like the two youngsters who had had the wits scared out of them by finding Fleming standing down there — he could have eluded them by simply stepping behind any of the huge old oaks and keeping out of sight until the riders had moved past.

As for the footprints, anyone would have seen they were leaving marks in the trail dust; all they'd have had to do to avoid that would be to climb over a fence and walk beside the trail through the grass.

When a brisk voice said, "Beautiful view, isn't it?" Fleming was not the least bit surprised. As he turned towards the old man's voice he agreed.

"Very beautiful, Mister Marchant." He studied the rawboned, erect figure in its cotton shirt and trousers. "Fine place for a man to commune with nature."

Old Marchant's face lifted with a sharp look. "The best way to commune with nature, Sergeant, is to get a hell of a long way off by yourself."

Fleming waited until Peter Marchant came up and halted a yard or two away. He watched the old man's narrowed gaze flick over the places Fleming had been studying. Then he said, "By any chance, Mister Marchant, do you own a pair of binoculars?"

Again the sharp look came and went as the older man turned his head towards Fleming. "Of course. I'll wager you can't find a person living in Forest Hills who doesn't own a pair. And that goes for the hired help." Marchant's expression changed slightly, grew a shade sardonic. "Unique thing about people, Sergeant. No one ever admits that their secret hobby is watching other people, and in the city sometimes it actually isn't, but you put people out in the country, even in a place as exalted as Forest Hills, and gradually they become snoops." The old grey eyes darkened with hard amusement. "They call it bird-watching."

Fleming smiled. It was not hard to respect old Marchant, but what Paul Fleming was beginning to feel was liking for the brusque, direct old loner. Not since he had been quite young had he known any men of this particular kind. In fact, he'd often thought that after the passing of his father and one particular uncle, the breed had become extinct. Now he knew there was still one left.

He didn't take the tactful approach with the father he'd taken with the son. He spoke to Peter Marchant the way he'd have spoken to his cantankerous uncle, dead now twelve years. He said, "Blassingame was fifty-five years old. Did you know that, Mister Marchant?" and when the older man shook his head, Fleming then said, "That's not old, if a man takes care of himself, and living alone could get lonely, even with all the money in the world — or maybe *because* of that."

Old Marchant's brow furrowed. "Women?" he said, then looked down his nose at Fleming. "Ridiculous. He wasn't the kind."

"No? A lot of men aren't the kind, Mister Marchant, until they see someone, maybe another man's wife, and the sparks begin to fly."

Marchant repeated it. "Ridiculous." Then he said, "You didn't come here to ask something like that."

Fleming's gaze brightened. "Didn't I? What *did* I come up here for?"

"You've already made it clear. You suspect *me*."

Fleming smiled again. "In a way, maybe, but not of murder. I think it's probable that you and Lamont Blassingame were quite a bit alike, and even if you didn't like him — which is just a guess — you'd still find him a lot easier to live around than the other neighbours; the hunt set, for example, or the cocktail set."

Peter Marchant's reply was direct. "That's a fair job of deduction, Sergeant. All right, specifically, what is it you suspect me of?"

Fleming said, "You know as well as I do, Mister Marchant. What did you see down there by the bridle path when you were looking through your binoculars the day Blassingame was shot?"

Peter Marchant stood a moment in craggy silence, then he jerked his head and turned. "Come along to my cottage and have a cup of tea, Sergeant. This time of day I take tea as a tonic. Come along."

CHAPTER 6

A FEW QUESTIONS,
A FEW ANSWERS

Paul Fleming did not like tea, had never liked it, and when he accepted the cup and saucer from Peter Marchant and considered how much like antique rust the tea in the cup looked, he decided that the things detectives were called upon to do in the pursuance of their civic obligations sometimes fell into the category of purest sacrifice.

Marchant's cottage was one of the most charming small residences Fleming had ever been in. It had bright and sparkling windows in every wall, excepting the east ones, the walls facing towards his son's majestic manor house; there the windows were neither numerous nor spacious, but in every other direction they were wide and long, with a view that resembled a mural in changing colour.

Peter Marchant had spared no expense. Although his house seemed to possess no more than possibly four rooms, it was spacious, immaculate, and had a sweeping sense of roominess and honesty; no one had tried to create an illusion with a carved screen or landscape paintings.

As the older man dropped into a chair in the sitting-room and tasted the tea, he cocked his head slightly and studied Fleming. Then he said, "You a married man, Sergeant?"

Fleming shook his head. "No." He tasted the tea. It was strong enough to melt nails. As he lowered the cup Marchant smiled at him.

"You don't have to drink it."

Fleming set the cup aside. "Mind if I smoke?"

"No. It's a rotten habit, but that's your prerogative. I'll get you an ashtray." As the older man arose he cast one of his quick, hawk-like stares at Fleming. "You are a deceptive man, Sergeant."

Fleming accepted the ashtray. "So I've been told." He tapped ash into the tray and raised his eyes, waiting for the older man to sit down again, to get back to why they were sitting there.

Marchant sighed, drained the last of his tea and said, "I very seldom have guests. I don't really mind terribly. My wife has been dead a long while, and I suppose I was never really what my daughter-in-law would term

60

an outgoing person. Still, it's nice to have someone here I've invited in."

Fleming took this as a kind of compliment; probably as close to a genuine compliment as Peter Marchant ever got. He put out the cigarette. He didn't actually need it anyway. And he waited.

Marchant's tough, clear grey gaze missed nothing. He said, "I wasn't watching birds, Sergeant. Sometimes I talk to them, and I'm always glad to see them in the trees, especially this time of year, but I scarcely know one kind from another."

Fleming was relieved that now, finally, they were round to it. "What *were* you watching, Mister Marchant?"

The older man's eyes wavered, but only for a second. "Well, as a matter of fact there is a youngster, a boy whose parents were divorced a couple of years ago, who rides the path occasionally. Sometimes, when I see him coming, through my binoculars, I tramp down and manage to meet him on the trail. We just talk."

Fleming thought he understood. "Did you see him the day Blassingame was killed?"

"No. I saw a man across the far fence moving up the trail in the grass."

Fleming nodded. "All right. Was he carrying something?"

"*Two* things," responded the older man. "Something that looked to me, from this

61

distance like a pair of short sticks, one in each hand." The grey eyes were steady. "Would that have been a dismantled rifle, Sergeant?"

It was entirely possible, so Fleming said, "Maybe. How good a look did you get at him, Mister Marchant?"

The older man pointed to a pair of binoculars on a small marble-topped end table. "Pretty good sets of lenses, Sergeant. If he'd looked up my way when he passed through sunlight I'd have been able to see his face. But he didn't look up this way except once in a while as he stopped to look all around, and every time he did that he stayed in the darkest shadows . . . I thought he might be some kind of hiker. Sometimes they come up the path. They aren't supposed to be in here at all, but most of them don't litter or cause trouble, so usually when I see them I look the other way."

Fleming said, "Man or boy?"

"Man. No question about that at all. About your size and slightly lighter in build. Perhaps between twenty-five and thirty-five years of age, although I could be off on that as much as ten years. I base it on the way he walked; free and easy, loose-jointed, well-coordinated." A smile flickered over Peter Marchant's face. "He didn't need a staff to help himself along."

"Describe him," said Fleming. "A little under six feet tall, maybe a hundred and fifty or sixty pounds . . . Take it from there, please."

Marchant's brow furrowed in recollection. "He was wearing a nondescript grey-brown suit, no tie, collar open, looked to be sun-tanned and quite fit. Brownish hair. That's about all I can tell you, Sergeant. I gave up watching him and went back to looking for the boy. I didn't see any sign of him and when I looked back I couldn't find the man either, so I went down to the stable. Much later, when I heard about Blassingame, I didn't put two and two together until some-one, I think it was my son, told me the details — that Monty had been shot while on his patio by someone who was probably over in the vicinity of the bridle trail."

Fleming had one question left. "Blassin-game was killed last week. Today is Satur-day of the following week. . . ."

Peter Marchant understood at once, and seemed to grow a little pensive before an-swering. "Sergeant, I felt fairly certain you people would turn him up, whoever he is, without my shred of information . . . You see, my daughter-in-law does not really approve of me, in some ways. Do you understand? Well, let me put it this way: if my picture were suddenly to appear in the newspapers as a police witness of sorts, Eleanor would die. In Forest Hills people simply do not see murderers, even through binoculars. It's not being done, Sergeant."

Fleming smiled. "Can you keep it from her now, Mister Marchant?"

The older man shot back his answer. "That's up to you, not me. Can you keep me out of the newspapers?"

Fleming thought so. At least for a while. He rose. "I'll do my damndest."

Peter Marchant ambled back outside upon the little shaded porch with Fleming, who turned and gazed down towards the stable where a woman in riding trousers and a loose-fitting pullover sweater was handing the reins of a saddled horse to a man Fleming thought would be Clyde Scruggs. At his side Marchant said, "Eleanor, my daughter-in-law."

Fleming nodded and moved towards the grass beyond the porch. Just before heading for the stable he said, "Mister Marchant, you've lived here quite a few years and you've seen them all. Which one did he look like?"

Without taking his eyes off the distant figure of the woman Marchant said, "That's easy, Sergeant. He could have been almost anyone from around here." The grey eyes swung. "I really wish I could do better than that."

They smiled, and Fleming went off, heading in the direction of the stable. He could see the bridle path the entire way down to the stable. He'd been gazing at it most of the time, in fact, since he'd been on the Marchants' hill, even from inside Peter Marchant's cottage, and something intrigued him: he had not seen Eleanor Marchant come up the trail nor turn off it towards the stable where she now stood, looking out where Fleming was moving along, with a faintly puzzled, faintly anxious expression on her smooth, quite patrician face.

Fleming smiled, slowed his gait until the horse-handler had led the ridden animal away to be cared for, then Fleming picked up his gait a little. The beautiful woman standing across a wash-rack watching his approach had a soft, wide mouth, clear blue eyes, hair the colour of fresh-spun gold, and a complexion that seemed to be as much the product of life-long health as heritage. Eleanor Whiting Marchant was undeniably a lovely woman.

She seemed to be perhaps thirty-five years of age, give or take a year or two, and, possibly because she had never borne children and was physically active, her figure was flawless.

As Fleming rummaged for his I.D. folder he thought detachedly that this was exactly the kind of woman a man worth millions would buy.

The blue eyes widened slightly at sight of

the badge, when sunlight bounced off it, then she moistened her lips in understanding, and Fleming could not tell whether her direct, steady gaze at him meant she was wary or whether it meant she resented Fleming's presence. Probably both, he decided, as he pocketed the folder and tried a tentative smile.

"Just a few routine questions," he murmured.

They were quite alone, in the shady area of the stable. It was pleasant there as Fleming leaned upon the planking that separated them. He thought Eleanor Whiting Marchant had to be one of the most thoroughly handsome women he had ever seen.

She said, "Right here, Sergeant? Wouldn't it be more appropriate at the house?"

Fleming smiled. "Right here is fine. I like the smell of barns."

"Do you?" murmured the soft, wide mouth, and Fleming sensed that he had just been dissected, categorised, and type-cast, and it did not bother him one bit.

"A beautiful day for a ride," he said, glancing past towards the trail.

Eleanor Marchant offered a mechanical smile. "A trifle warm. What can I do for you, Sergeant?"

Fleming brought his gaze back to the patrician features. "I'm interested in the Blassingame matter, Mrs Marchant. I spoke to your husband earlier."

She said, "Did you?" in a serene and totally disinterested tone of voice. "I'm sorry I missed you, but I went out before the heat came."

Fleming nodded sympathetically. "It's a beautiful bridle path, though; lots of shade along it, I rather imagine."

The lovely woman turned slightly to look back. "It's a nice ride," she admitted non-committally, then faced Fleming again. "I enjoyed it this morning."

Fleming did not meet her gaze for a moment. *Lie number one; she hadn't been on the bridle path or he'd have seen her.* He brought up the professional smile again. "Anything you could tell me about Mister Blassingame would be appreciated, Mrs Marchant."

She gave Fleming a clear-eyed stare. "I? Frankly, Sergeant, I'm probably the least likely person to talk to about Monty Blassingame in the entire community."

"You didn't care for him, then?"

She almost looked away, but pulled her gaze back and held it steady when she answered. "No, to be very honest with you, I didn't like Monty. Not too many people did. But I was completely flabbergasted when he was killed."

Fleming was sympathetic. "No one disliked

67

him *that* much, eh?"

The soft, lovely mouth said, "Exactly. Monty Blassingame was — well, at times anyway — crude and rude. I never really knew what he'd say next, and that can be devastating."

Fleming turned the word over and over in his mind and never quite came to grips with it in this context, but then he was neither a woman nor a very socially prominent man either, so in his particular world people rarely used the word 'devastating', unless they meant the result of an earthquake or something similar — perhaps a tidal wave or a shower of fragmented comets.

"At the few affairs you attended," said Fleming, adjusting his vocabulary to this lovely woman, "who in particular did Mister Blassingame seem to pay the most attention to?"

Eleanor Marchant did not even hesitate when she replied. "The bar, Sergeant."

Fleming smiled. "Even when he danced, Mrs Marchant?"

"Well, actually, Monty did not like to dance . . . which was just as well, really, because he was not very good at it, and frankly, I don't believe he ever danced with the same woman twice . . . Really, Sergeant, I simply can't help you as much as I wish I could."

"The day he was killed," said Fleming, unwilling to let her go quite yet. "By any chance were you out riding?"

"No. I drove into the city with my husband that morning and we did not get back until late evening." The blue eyes settled like still stone upon Fleming. "Do you suspect me, Sergeant?"

"Not for a moment," said Fleming. "I just wondered if by any chance you were riding, and might have heard the report of a gun." He straightened up. "I won't hold you any longer. Thank you, Mrs Marchant."

She nodded, turned and went walking briskly towards the far end of the stable compound where the path led uphill towards the manor house. Fleming leaned and watched. She was indeed a very beautiful woman — but, somehow, not desirable. At least not desirable to Paul Fleming, and it had nothing to do with the fact that she had lied to him.

CHAPTER 7

A MATTER OF ASSOCIATES

Fleming was vague about the designation 'investment banker', but it sounded impressively lofty, which it probably was in the case of Clarence Dunning if one could judge by his estate.

Fleming could have gone somewhere and telephoned to Mike Sublette, but it wasn't all that important what an 'investment banker' was. Not at the moment, anyway.

Dunning's estate, southward of the Blassingame place, was closer to the southward entrance to Forest Hills. In fact, from out front of the Dunning residence, by looking southward and eastward a little, those twin stone pillars were visible.

Like all the houses, at least all the houses Fleming had visited lately in Forest Hills, the Dunning residence sat atop a low hill. But the Dunning home had a wider hill. In fact, the tennis courts and even the small stable were also both atop the hill, instead of being slightly below it on the rearward slope as was true with the Blassingame and Marchant outbuildings.

Dunning's house was different too. Instead of being entirely of rich, golden fieldstone like the Marchant place, or of half fieldstone and half wood, like the Blassingame residence, the Dunning house had thick-butt shakes on the roof, a low, sweeping elevation, and a quite wide verandah called a *ramada* which ran completely around the house. There could be no mistaking the wealth of the people who lived in this house, if for no other reason than because it was inside Forest Hills' gates, but the impression was actually not so much of money as of quiet comfort and charm.

Fleming, who was becoming almost unconsciously something of a Forest Hills architectural *afficionado*, decided that he liked the Dunning place best, so far.

When the servant took him round back on the verandah, paved the entire way with hand-made red brick set in rough grout to increase the charm, Fleming decided idly that when he made his first million he would have a place just like this; but not in Forest Hills, closer to his work. He smiled to himself, and when the servant halted to introduce Sergeant Fleming to Clarence Dunning, round back where the investment banker had been reading, Fleming smiled without the least effort because he was already in a smiling mood.

Dunning was a greying man with a tanned, fit look, quick, piercing blue eyes, who exuded an aura of physical and mental well-being. He had the smooth face of a twenty-five-year-old, but his hair, the look in his eyes, and a rather general impression one got, suggested he was closer to forty.

There was a tennis racket near where Dunning had been sitting, which seemed to account for Dunning's slight appearance of red-faced recovery. As soon as Dunning had shaken hands he drew up a chair at the little metal table where he had been sitting and offered Fleming a chilled drink, something with gin in it, Dunning suggested. Fleming declined and lit a smoke instead. As the servant departed Dunning said, "I've been wondering, Sergeant; seemed I was being slighted. After all, I do live just south of Blassingame." Dunning smiled. He had perfect teeth and a charming smile. Fleming exhaled smoke, sat in the shade of the wide verandah, and looked westward, then to the north-west where the scenery seemed to flow with an unending green variety of tranquility.

Fleming said, "There didn't seem to be any hurry," and brought his gaze back to study the man beside him in the shade.

Dunning said, "Of course I'll be glad to help in any way that I can," and turned to murmur thanks to the servant who had returned with an iced drink in a chilled glass. "But as a matter of fact, Sergeant, Monty and I were not very close."

Fleming nodded acceptance of this. "He didn't seem to be very close to anyone."

Dunning sampled his drink, and it was odd how just hearing the ice clink in the glass made Fleming actually feel cooler. Dunning lowered the glass. "You've probably heard it all, Sergeant," he said. "At times Monty was rather forthright. There were a number of things he was not fond of." Dunning chuckled. "One time years ago he told me there was no such thing as a completely honest and ethical human being."

Fleming smiled to himself; if Blassingame had been able to arrive at this conclusion by avoiding people, Fleming wondered what he would have thought if he could have been a policeman for a few months.

Dunning said, "Actually, Monty was harmless. He didn't force himself on people. If they left him alone, he left them alone."

Fleming stopped studying the countryside beyond the verandah and gazed again at his host. "Not exactly the type to be murdered, was he?" he said. "That's where the main obstacle appears, Mister Dunning."

The investment banker closed both palms

73

around his frosted highball glass as he said, "Of course, something like this is entirely out of my line, Sergeant, but after all it happened next door, and a person can't help but wonder. Isn't it possible the killer was one of those unwashed, hippie-types; those revolutionists or whatever they're called?"

Fleming nodded. "Possibly." He did not bother explaining why he did not believe this; he wasn't there to enlighten Dunning, or to reason with the man. He was there to appraise and to listen.

"It could also have been robbery, couldn't it, Sergeant?"

Fleming thought about this question for a moment before answering. "Nothing appears to have been taken, Mister Dunning. That's the first thing I went over with Mister Blassingame's domestics. They said that as far as they knew nothing had been touched."

"Well then, that brings us back to the psychopath, doesn't it? Every time you pick up a newspaper there's an account of some senseless act of violence. Like this latest fad of renting safety-deposit boxes in banks, then putting time-bombs in them. Or driving the streets at night and indiscriminately sniping at lighted windows with high-powered rifles. Sergeant, at the risk of sounding like Monty Blassingame, it appears to me that something is dreadfully wrong with society these days."

This was also something Paul Fleming knew something about, but he felt no compulsion to discuss it with Clarence Dunning, so he said, "Did you, by any chance, have any business dealings with Lamont Blassingame?"

Dunning finished his highball before answering. "Not exactly. I'm chairman of the board of an electronics company Blassingame owned a good bit of stock in, and we shared an interest in shares and a few speculative operations, but not as associates. Now and then we'd meet, at the hunt club or over on the golf course, we talked a little of business, but you couldn't really say we had business dealings."

"Then your association with him," said Fleming, "would be social, as far as it went."

Dunning sighed and crossed his legs. "Yes. As far as it went."

Fleming couldn't see the Blassingame house from Clarence Dunning's rear patio, but he could trace out the winding course of the bridle path; evidently, when the developers of Forest Hills had laid the place out they had done so in such a way that every estate had access to the trail. Horseback riding, like tennis and swimming, evidently had meant the 'good life' to Forest Hills' developers. Golf too, but this was the first time Fleming had heard it mentioned that

75

there was a golf course. It did not surprise him.

Dunning broke the little silence by saying, "You probably realise everyone in Forest Hills hopes you solve this thing soon, Sergeant, so that it'll die out and be forgotten." Dunning smiled. "Our public image up here is built around the solid virtues. Murder doesn't help it at all."

Fleming rose. He was beginning to have an idea about something, and the public image of Forest Hills had nothing to do with it. Nor could he work up much sympathy for the Forest Hills image. "You will all survive," he told Clarence Dunning. "These things come and go, take my word for it."

Dunning also stood up. He was an inch or two taller than Paul Fleming, which made him six feet tall, or perhaps an inch taller. He was a trim, athletic man. As he turned to stroll back round front where Fleming had left his car, Dunning said, "Frankly, I'm at a loss, Sergeant. Unless it was one of those pointless things, or unless Monty's domestics were involved, I simply can't imagine why someone would want to kill him."

This was something Paul Fleming could agree with. "Maybe you're right about the psychopathic killer, Mister Dunning, but for my reputation's sake I hope not, because a murder without a motive is almost impossible to solve."

They parted at the car. Fleming drove on around the paved, private road back towards the main thoroughfare, and turned left to cruise farther up into the Forest Hills preserve than he had driven before. When he eventually found the golf course it was about as he might have expected it to be. The fields were emerald green, as smooth and perfectly maintained as they should have been, and the clubhouse was one of those long, low, delightful places in a setting of giant trees, where windows formed three-quarters of the entire front wall. Without appearing to have cost a great deal of money the clubhouse, Fleming felt certain, had probably cost only slightly less than the magnificent Marchant mansion.

He paused at the roadside to watch a threesome play through, and it was difficult to tell, at least from their attire, which were the caddies and which were the golf club members.

He finally drove in and parked, strolled out along the shaded front verandah, and when a genial man with curly hair appeared from within the building Fleming was prepared; if for no other reason than because he was wearing a tie and a suit instead of a sport shirt and a sport jacket, he stood out.

The curly-headed man exuded charm as he walked up and said, "Could I be of any help?"

Fleming did not return the man's smile; he was going to be asked to leave, of course. He was going to be told in the most charming way that the club was private. He dug out his I.D. folder and showed it to the man, and the charm dwindled just a little, the genial brown eyes became slightly masked with caution. The man said, "I see," in a different tone of voice. "Well, I suppose we could talk in my office, Sergeant. It'll be about the Blassingame thing, of course."

Fleming stood and gazed out where the golfers were, and said, "I don't think we have to go inside, and I won't have to take much of your time." He did not ask the man his name. "Tell me, did Mister Blassingame play much golf?"

The curly-headed man did not take his eyes off Fleming's profile. "Very rarely. In fact, in the five years I've been manager here, I can only recall Mister Blassingame being here once or twice."

That was interesting. Fleming stopped watching the players and turned. "Do you by any chance keep some kind of ledger — some kind of daily tally of who plays?"

"Yes, of course we do. Would you like to see it?"

Fleming finally smiled. "No; not unless you can remember the specific days when Blassingame played here."

The curly-headed man looked rueful. "Sergeant, that would have to go back several years. I know for a fact he hasn't been out here in the past couple of years. He really wasn't the golfing type."

"Could you, by any chance, look up in your tallybook and find the days that he played?"

"I suppose so," replied the golf club manager, and did not look too pleased at being saddled with this obligation. "It would take some time, though."

Fleming kept smiling. He even offered his hand. "I was sure you'd co-operate," he said, and shook, then turned to leave. "I'll drop by again in a day or two. I'd like to see those entries."

By the time Fleming got back to his car the curly-headed man had gone back inside. Fleming grunted to himself. It was probably necessary for these people to guard their exclusiveness, but still and all, it was irritating at times to be pounced on, even though the pouncer was all smiles and geniality, as though one were a leper.

Fleming drove back slowly the way he had come, and near the whitewashed stone pillars that marked the entrance to exclusive and private Forest Hills, he looked up at the hilltop home of Clarence Dunning, then he left the area and began breathing the less lofty air of the world beyond.

CHAPTER 8

MISS MAITLAND

Sublette said, "Dunning, according to my information, is one of those people who can smell something dying. He'll be around as soon as a company is in trouble to make an offer to re-finance, then, because a company that's going under has no choice, when he's dangling salvation in front of the company's nose, he tosses down his ultimatum: either they appoint him president or chairman of the board, or he withdraws his offer." Sublette made a little gesture of finality. "That's what an investment banker is; at least, that's what *his* kind of an investment banker is."

Fleming blew smoke at the ceiling of Sublette's office. It was Monday morning and Fleming had been doing a little pondering over the week-end. "Did Dunning ever make a bad guess? Did he ever drop a bundle because someone out-smarted him?"

Mike Sublette shook his head. "If you're thinking of Lamont Blassingame — no."

"How about Richard or Peter Marchant?"

"Not in the same league," replied Sublette. "The people Dunning goes for are the borderline cases. Like I said, he can smell 'em dying. The Marchants already had it made and salted away before Dunning appeared on the scene. At least, I can't find any connection, and I went back five years through the Securities and Exchange Commission."

Sublette dug through the papers atop his desk and picked up one that appeared to be a photographic copy of some kind. "When you asked if Dunning ever dropped a bundle I almost said that he had, but actually it's not a lost cause — yet." Sublette leaned to offer Fleming the photostat copy. "That's something I picked up Friday; as you can see, Paul, Dunning departed from his usual procedure. What interested me was that in all the cases I've investigated of his over the past five years, that loan to the Davis-Whiting Manufacturing Corporation is the only time he did not insist on being appointed president or chairman of the board before handing over the cash."

Fleming leaned to squash his cigarette and with a perfectly blank face he read the recorded copy of Dunning's loan to a Virginia corporation involved with federal contracts, called Davis-Whiting. The corporation had two factories and its main offices in Richmond, Virginia.

Fleming carefully pocketed this paper and got to his feet. "Anything else?"

Sublette looked at the mess atop his desk as though expecting something to suddenly appear there, then he said, "Not at the moment. What did you dig up on the Marchants?"

"Not even a hint of trouble, anywhere. No connection with Blassingame, business or otherwise. Like you just said, they were in a different league from Blassingame."

Mike stood up. "That lawyer for the Blassingame estate called just before I left Friday, Paul. He said Blassingame's heir would be out there at Forest Hills today, right after she made arrangements for the funeral. The lawyer sounded as though he wanted you to be there, too."

Fleming was quite agreeable. But in fact it had been his intention to drive to Forest Hills anyway. He thanked Sublette and left the building. On the drive out he decided there wouldn't be anything very startling Elisabeth Maitland could tell him, so he was lukewarm about the meeting. She hadn't been in the country in four years or so, and from what Fleming had deduced about Lamont Blassingame's disposition and personality, he was not the type to write Nervous Nelly letters to a niece, even had he suspected someone might try to kill him.

For these reasons, although Fleming saw the shiny car up there out front of the Blassingame residence when he finally reached Forest Hills, he drove right on past and did not stop until he was in the gravelled parking area out front of the golf club.

The curly-headed, genial manager greeted Fleming with a hint of subdued affability. "It was one hell of a job," he said, taking Fleming to a handsome, very modern office and pointing to a large table where a number of loose-leaf binders lay, two of them opened, the others closed and untidily stacked.

The manager had red-pencilled both the daily entries denoting that Lamont Blassingame had played golf on those dates. One entry was four years previous, one was three years previous. Fleming baffled the curly-headed man by simply verifying that Blassingame's signature was there, then he slowly ran a finger up and down both sheets of paper, not once, but twice, and finally, as he flicked open the binders to extract both pages, he said, "I'll give you a receipt for these things; I'd like to borrow them for a while." He was already folding the pages to fit his inside jacket pocket.

The curly-headed man was flustered. "I'm not sure what club policy has to say about this sort of thing. It's never happened before, since I've been here."

Fleming smiled and offered his hand. As the curly-headed man shook, looking mildly worried, Fleming soothed him. "I'll have them back in a week or so. I appreciate your co-operation very much."

Later, Fleming strolled down the tiled patio outside and stood a while looking out over the empty greens and fairways. Even though a man would never be able to play golf in a place like this, there was something soul-satisfying about just standing there looking out where sunshine and blue skies and high treetops contributed to the beauty of a de-lightful setting. Then he went back, got into his car and drove down to the Blassingame place.

Elisabeth Maitland was a thorough shock. Fleming hadn't actually speculated, he'd had other things on his mind, but when Larkin took him to the beautiful study and introduced him to the woman sitting at Lamont Blassingame's desk, the unflappa-ble sergeant of detectives looked long and quietly as he inclined his head at the intro-duction, then entered the room at the Mait-land woman's request, but did not accept the chair she offered.

She was perhaps as old as Eleanor Mar-chant. No older, though, and where Mrs Marchant was fair and golden and soft and

84

creamy, Elisabeth Maitland had dark eyes, red-brown dark hair, skin the colour of new copper, a few shades lighter perhaps, and the features of a Greek goddess. She no more resembled her late uncle than Fleming himself did.

When she stood up behind the desk, that was another revelation. Fleming had difficulty accepting the fact that this very beautiful and voluptuous woman would bury herself in some god-forsaken jungle. She smiled and told Fleming of her conversation with Eric Frederickson, of Frederickson, Martin & Bishop. He listened without heeding, then he turned and went to take that chair she had offered. He unconsciously reached for his packet of smokes. In fact, he lit up and exhaled before he remembered that he should have asked permission first. But the beautiful nurse got an ashtray off the fireplace mantel, brought it over and leaned to put it atop the small rose-wood table at his elbow. When she leaned, Fleming could hardly have avoided noticing how large and firm she was. Their eyes met briefly, then she returned behind the desk as she said, "It was such a complete shock. We'd just completed a vaccination clinic out back and had been back at the hospital an hour or so when the boy came bicycling up with Mister Frederickson's cable. I was stunned; more so, Sergeant Fleming, when

85

I got the details." The liquid dark eyes probed Fleming's face. "I just can't imagine anything like this happening to my uncle."

Fleming said, "Why not, Miss Maitland?" and that seemed to throw her off balance even more. "From what I can learn, your uncle wouldn't have won any popularity contests."

Her dark eyes flashed at Fleming. "Perhaps not, but neither would he have harmed anyone, Sergeant. He was always a unique individual. I can remember instances when my parents were still alive, that my father would have a fit if he knew my mother's brother was coming to visit. I suppose that was a common reaction, but he was always wonderful to me, and how does one judge people, Sergeant, by what other people think or say about them, or by how *they* are treated?"

Fleming thought that was about right. "By how he treated you, of course, Miss Maitland, but from where I sit he was a different man."

"Different enough for someone to want to kill him, Sergeant?"

Fleming blew smoke as he replied. "I don't know. I know someone *did* kill him, but whether they killed him because they did not like him, or for some other reason, I can't say." He put out his cigarette. Her eyes followed every move he made. When he leaned back and got comfortable again, he finally smiled at her. "What can you tell me, Miss Maitland?"

"About my uncle? Well, you probably know by now that I've been out of the country for about four years. He came to Thailand my first year over there, and spent a week with me. I think his intention was to try and talk me into coming home, but all he said, as I saw him to the airport, was that whenever I'd had enough to cable him and he'd send whatever I needed to return. We wrote, now and then, while I was in Thailand, but when I went over to Cambodia sometimes I didn't get the time, so our correspondence got to be rather patchy."

"When were you planning on returning?" asked Fleming.

"Next year. I'd agreed to sign over for two terms of two and a half years each. My contract would have expired next summer."

"In your correspondence with your uncle," asked Fleming, "did he send you the local news and so forth?"

Elisabeth Maitland settled both elbows atop the desk and rested her face in both palms. "If a horse got sick, or if he saw in the newspapers where someone I'd mentioned knowing in college, some old friend perhaps, got married, things like that." The beautiful dark eyes lingered on Fleming. "Is that what you mean, or have I missed the point?"

Fleming laughed and stood up, ready to depart. "You missed the point, but if I prompted you, then it couldn't be much of a recollection, could it?"

She also rose. "I'm not sure I understand, Sergeant. There is something I'm supposed to know?"

He crossed to the door, shaking his head. "Never mind. Incidentally, are you going to stay here, at the estate?"

She walked along beside him, looking down. "I had been thinking about it. Mister Frederickson asked the same thing." She looked up suddenly. "What do you think?"

"By all means stay," said Fleming. "If you're worried about lightning striking the same place twice, I don't think there's much ground for anxiety on that score. The person who shot your uncle wasn't just out winging people. He had his reason, good or bad."

As they stepped forth into the outdoors sunshine and Fleming squinted to look left and right, the beautiful woman went as far as the car with him, and leaned down after he had got in.

"You don't volunteer much information, do you, Sergeant?"

He smiled out at her. "Even if I had much to volunteer, Miss Maitland. I appreciate your co-operation."

She kept looking at him. "I was no help. You don't have to tell me that. Mister Frederickson said you would probably want permission to examine my uncle's records, as well as the matters pertaining to the estate."

Fleming said, "And he advised against it. Right?"

The dark eyes twinkled. "Right. But if you want to look, you have my permission."

Fleming thanked her, started the car and drove away. As before, he did not turn right which would have taken him down past the Dunning estate to the stone pillars and out beyond Forest Hills. He instead turned left and drove about a mile up-country, then slowly began making as near to a parallel run beside the bridle trail as he could.

There were times when he could not drive within a half-mile or more of it, but he never lost sight of it, and that was what he wanted. He back-tracked it to the point of origin — out back of the Forest Hills estates' westerly stone-pillared access road. From there all around and through the miles of country-side where it meandered seemingly without direction, then, after passing or bisecting every estate, it wound back around and eventually came full circle, in the area out back of the west Forest Hills entrance.

When he had the lay of the bridle path well in mind, Fleming drove slowly back to the

Marchant place, and this time he did not go to the front door at all, but ambled round back in the direction of the lovely cottage of the elder Marchant.

Two people had lied to him, so far, and what Fleming needed now was for at least one more person to tell him a lie.

CHAPTER 9

A HIKE IN THE SUNSHINE

Peter Marchant was not at his cottage, he was on down the hill a short distance at the stable. It was Clyde Scruggs' day off, he told Fleming, offering a smile as though they were old friends instead of acquaintances through a dubious connection. "The Larkins take Thursday off and Clyde takes Monday off," said Peter Marchant, stretching a soaking horseblanket over a long pole out front of the stable. "Personally, I think Scruggs gets the best of it; Sunday and Monday off in consecutive order is better than two days off half a week apart, eh, Sergeant?"

Fleming thought that it probably was. He could have added that days off were not his strong suit, but instead he asked a question. "That day Blassingame died, and you were watching the bridle path — by any chance was there a rider anywhere within sight?"

Marchant finished arranging the blanket,

then leaned upon the pole and squinted at Fleming. "Not that I saw. And I was searching for one." The older man clearly wanted to ask a question, too, but he did not do it. He straightened up and turned to make certain the blanket had no wrinkles in it.

"And the times you go hiking," said Fleming, standing in hay-scented shade, "have you ever seen a man who resembled that man you saw the day of the killing, also out hiking?"

Marchant paused long enough to frown. He seemed to sense Fleming's questions had more of a purpose this time; he seemed to want to give exact answers. "Sergeant," he eventually replied, speaking slowly, "I see other people out hiking almost every time I go meandering, and yes, I'm sure some of them were about the same general build as the man carrying the disassembled rifle. But I can't right offhand remember thinking there was such a similarity. I mean afterwards, when I got to thinking back."

Fleming didn't care. That was not why he was asking these questions. But he *did* care about the answer to his next question.

"If riders don't stay on the trail, Mister Marchant, where do they go? I'm thinking that you probably do more tramping the hills than anyone else, so maybe you'd have seen someone riding off the trail, or perhaps know where they might go."

The old man shot Fleming a wry look. "You're full of questions today, aren't you? Yes, I see people off the path very often. Some people prefer riding on their own land, particularly if they're training a young horse. Mostly, pleasure-riders stay on the trail, though. As for where those people might go," old Marchant threw up an arm, "anywhere they feel like going, Sergeant. There are a number of beautiful, secluded spots in these hills. There are also a number of small lakes — some aren't so small. I've seen people having picnics at most of them."

Fleming had been looking past, around the full flank of the slope down towards the bridle path, and beyond, over into the grounds of the Blassingame estate. Farther, in fact quite a bit farther, he could make out the north side and part of the back of the Dunning house, but it was nearly blocked from sight by the rolling countryside.

Old Marchant stepped to a canvas-backed chair and sat down. He kept looking up towards the mansion of his son and daughter-in-law, only the upper half of which was visible over the rounded rise and top-off of the slope.

"You're making some headway," he mumbled, without looking at Fleming. "Or else you're considering buying property around here. More than an hour ago I saw you driving around keeping close to the bridle trail." The old man turned his head. "Who's the dark-haired woman at the Blassingame place?"

Fleming almost smiled. It was evidently especially true what Marchant had said about people being put down in the country with nothing else to do, taking up neighbour-watching as a pastime; it was evidently especially true of Peter Marchant.

"Blassingame's niece," said Fleming, "and heir."

Old Marchant's eyes widened. "Is that so? I didn't know he had a niece."

"She's been a nurse in Asia for the past four years. Her name is Elisabeth Maitland."

Marchant digested all this and grunted. "With all the sick people in this country, why do they get this notion that they have to go somewhere else and do their good works?"

This time Fleming did smile. "You could ask her, she's very friendly. One more question: west from here is there a place — maybe one of those ponds you mentioned — where people would go to have a picnic, or to perhaps just meet and maybe kill the time?"

The older man replied promptly. "About a half or maybe three-quarters of a mile slightly south and west, there is no pond, but there's a beautiful little glade. It's down where the bridle path turns southerly, so most riders don't go there because there are

no gates off the path at that place."

"How would a person reach it from here asked Fleming, and Peter Marchant ros beckoned, and led the way to the far end the stable where nothing hindered the viev There, he pointed with an upraised arm.

"Do you see where the path bends toward the south? Well, the glade is just abou north from where that bend is. Do you se those great trees? The glade is about fift yards north of them. In fact, those trees completely surround the glade. It's like being a thousand miles from civilisation, in that pleasant little place."

Fleming was only half-listening. He was tracing out some of those white board fences. In the direction of the trees Marchant had mentioned, one of those fences followed out the lift and rise of the countryside down at a lower elevation. He asked about the fence.

"My son's property is on this side," Marchant explained. "There's a gate down there, about mid-way. There is also another gate over in the fence that parallels the bridle trail."

That was what Fleming had had in mind walking down there to verify. Now he did not have to make the hike. But out of a clear blue sky Peter Marchant nudged him and said, "I was thinking of taking a walk dow there, when you came along, Sergean

Come along, you can accompany me." When Fleming gauged the distance, and the fact that all the way back they would be walking uphill, old Marchant gave a scornful grunt. "Good heavens, you're half my age. If I can enjoy that, you surely should. Come along."

Fleming went, but first he pulled loose his tie and stuffed it in a pocket, and mid-way down the far slope he began to wish he'd left his jacket behind at the stable.

It was hot on the grassy hillside. It was also humid the way Fleming remembered many summer days in the north-west where he had matured. Humidity up there meant a summer thundershower, but within a hundred miles of Los Angeles in any direction it simply meant — humidity.

Peter Marchant did not take big strides, but he obviously could have if he'd been hurrying. As they routed a meadowlark and two noisy little kildeers Marchant said, "I started out a farm boy in Nebraska, Sergeant." The tough grey eyes rested a moment on Fleming, then swung ahead again. "I used to do this — just go adventuring out across the prairie. Of course that *was* prairie, and this — well, hell — this is an improvised hothouse. But still, the air tastes the same and the grass and trees and bushes smell about the same. What I'm telling you, Sergeant, is that if you live long enough you'll come full circle. Here I am, back

tramping the grasslands."

Fleming said, "With two differences."

The old man looked at him, then suddenly smiled. "Yeah. The money, and the years that have slipped away. I regret the years. The money: I never went after it because I needed it to do anything for my ego. I went after it to satisfy a hunter's urge. That's all. I don't care about it. I never cared very much about it."

Fleming did not speak. It seemed to him that once a man had millions, or at least had had them, and still had all the funds he could possibly ever want, it was easy to act contemptuous about wealth. But he was not walking across the grassy slope under a golden, blazing sun, and perspiring like a studhorse in a pasture full of mares, because he wanted to exchange ideas or philosophies with Peter Marchant.

Finally, they got down to the white fence. The older man stopped, smiled at Fleming and turned to start northward, paralleling the fence. "Gate's up here a short distance," he said.

They found it. Fleming managed to be beside the older man when they reached the gate. He reached first, and then stepped up to slide back the wooden latch. Whatever he had hoped to discover was not visible. He would just have to assume someone else had recently opened this gate. As they passed through and Fleming closed the gate afterwards, he asked whose property they were on.

Marchant said, "It's a kind of a Jonah. The development company still owns it. You see, most of the surrounding estates are on high ground, and no one wanted to buy down here and not have much of a view, so the land belongs to the developers. There is another drawback; every winter that we have a cloudburst, all the run-off water rushes down here."

They made their way through several tiers of great, shaggy old trees. Birds scolded them unmercifully. Marchant did not so much as look up or look back. He obviously knew every yard of ground through here.

Fleming saw marks on the spongy ground where a rider had passed through following this same trail not too long before; *how* long he would not hazard a guess even to himself.

Marchant stepped forth into the glade and waited. As soon as Fleming came out and paused to look around, Marchant smiled. "Secluded," he said. "Ideal place for a picnic, for just about anything. My son thought of buying it for a while, simply in order to have a little more pasture for the horses. He changed his mind," said the older man, and struck off to take Fleming on an exploratory trip Fleming did not feel much need for. He was in good enough physical shape for all this, but he hadn't really been prepared, nor conditioned, for a hike when he'd arrived at the Marchant residence an hour or so earlier.

The glade was very quiet and fragrant and attractive. It also seemed to have visitors from time to time. Mostly afoot, evidently, because there was scarcely any sign that horses had been in here.

When he had seen enough, Fleming suggested that they go back. Peter Marchant was perfectly willing, but he had an aversion to returning by the same trail he had used to arrive at a place, so he struck off on an angling course that carried them to the top of the slope by a rather circuitous, unnecessarily prolonged route. When they reached the Marchant stable again, Fleming had to sit down and spend ten full minutes picking itchy little foxtails and cockle burrs from his socks. Peter Marchant hiked on, right on up the slope to his cottage, and eventually returned with two bottles of cold, golden beer. For the first time since he could recall, Fleming drank on duty. His conscience did not bother him in the slightest.

Peter Marchant watched the foxtail and burr picking for a while, then said, "The last time you were here, Sergeant, my son and daughter-in-law didn't much like the idea."

Fleming said nothing, but he could believe they hadn't liked it.

"In fact, my daughter-in-law does not really care too much for detectives. Not you in particular — just detectives. She is mortally afraid of adverse publicity. They told me that if you returned I was to refer you to the company of family barristers, and not to say two words to you."

Fleming finished with the socks and went to work putting his shoes back on and tying them. He cocked his head a little at the tough-faced older man. "They have seen my car out front by now, Mister Marchant, and I imagine they could see us walking down to the glade."

Marchant smiled serenely. "Not today, Sergeant. They are in the city for some political banquet, something like that. The reason I mentioned this was so that you would not inadvertently spill the beans the next time you see them. Understand?"

Fleming said, "Understand," and got to his feet. He smelled of weeds and crushed grass and masculine perspiration. He thanked Peter Marchant for his time and went plodding on up the rest of the hill past the cottage towards the main house with his tie off and his jacket slung over his shoulder — smiling to himself.

CHAPTER 10

A SHOCKER FOR FLEMING

Two days later Fleming made it a point to encounter Richard Marchant, and under circumstances that resolved something that interested Fleming. Everyone in Forest Hills appeared to own horses, as though it were some mark of distinction, which it could have been for all Fleming knew — or cared — but this was the first time he had ever seen Richard Marchant riding a horse.

Fleming was up near the main thoroughfare leading through the estate community gazing downwards where the trail meandered when he saw the rider coming, alone and slowly. He had no idea who the rider was until young Marchant was near enough to be recognised.

As they met, Richard Marchant nodded at Fleming with no indication of pleasure and said, "Good morning. It's one of those days when people have to be outside, isn't it?"

Fleming agreed. "If there's a reason for living, I suppose someone will discover it, someday, sitting under a tree on a day like this."

Marchant put a sharp glance downward. "A detective-philosopher, Sergeant?"

"Just a detective," replied Fleming.

Marchant obviously did not care much for this interruption nor, Fleming felt sure, the cause of it. But he did not lift his reins or knee his horse to move along. Instead, he said, "It seems to me that things are dragging a bit, Sergeant." He was obviously referring to the Blassingame murder.

Fleming cordially agreed with him. "It does seem that way. But my business isn't like most businesses, Mister Marchant. I don't deal with people who need my goods or services; I deal almost exclusively with people who do *not* co-operate."

Marchant's brows arched. "Here," he said, "in Forest Hills?" He made it sound as though he equated Forest Hills with the afterlife Paradise.

Fleming was not to be diverted from what he had in mind, even though he thought of a rough answer to Marchant. He had been considering a visit to Richard Marchant the night before, but without any set schedule. Now that they were together, Fleming took advantage of it. Accidental meetings were usually so much more productive than scheduled meetings.

He used Marchant's last remark, his implication that Forest Hills was a superior place, to get their conversation on a level where he could direct it.

"Not that I've encountered any active resistance in Forest Hills," he said, gazing upwards at the man on the horse. "Just a little inadvertent misapprehension, is about all."

Marchant was interested. "That's hard to believe, Sergeant. By now everyone knows who you arc and that thc sooncr you're finished here the sooner this unwelcome newspaper publicity will stop."

"Of course, my being finished here doesn't necessarily mean I'll tag a murderer, does it, Mister Marchant?" said Fleming. "I suppose just seeing me leave and the publicity die is actually all people want."

Marchant's eyes flashed. "Nonsense, Sergeant. As far as I know, everyone would like very much to have you make your arrest, or whatever it is that you do, and end this affair properly."

Fleming smiled as though this comforted him, then he said, "This is the first time I've seen you out riding, Mister Marchant. I met your wife a few days ago as she returned from a ride. Come to think of it, I've never seen your father ride."

Marchant studied Fleming closely as he replied. "My father is an old man. Riding makes him stiff and uncomfortable for a few days afterwards. Anyway, he's a lifelong and inveterate hiker — as you've no doubt observed."

Fleming said, "Yes, indeed. In fact, I believe he was out hiking the day Blassingame was killed."

Marchant's reaction was swift. "No, I don't believe that he was. As I recall, Sergeant, that was the day he worked around the stables. He has quite a fondness for being down there. I'm fairly sure he did not go hiking the day Monty was shot."

Fleming shrugged. Marchant's defence of his father had been too quick, too fiercely protective. And if Marchant had thought about it, he surely would have guessed that Fleming would have already ascertained whether or not the old man had been hiking that day; Fleming had done the same for everyone else — ascertained their whereabouts the day of the murder. Why had Marchant been so quick to the defence?

Fleming glanced at his watch as he said, "You're probably right, Mister Marchant, and I won't keep you any longer." He looked up, smiling. "It's been pleasant talking to you."

Marchant lifted his reins and rode on, and Fleming's last look at his face showed a worried horseman. None of these people were fools; whether they could actually second-guess Paul Fleming or not, they were certainly shrewd enough to sense shades and shifts, not only in words but in looks.

Fleming returned to his car, ran up the engine, then put in a call to Mike Sublette in the city. The distance was too great for good transmission or reception, so the call had to be routed through an outlying sheriff's department sub-station, and that slowed things considerably.

By the time Fleming had told Sublette what he wanted, although the bridle path paralleled the main thoroughfare some little distance in this area, Richard Marchant, riding at a walk, had finally gone out of sight. Still, delayed transmission or not, Fleming was satisfied when he eventually stopped the car's engine and sat back in the pleasant day to have a smoke and continue to gaze westerly, down where the bridle path lay in inviting shade between its paralleling white board fences.

A small, shiny car pulled in beside him and a smiling, quite handsome pair of dark eyes looked over. Fleming smiled back as Elisabeth Maitland said, "Beautiful day for solitary meditation, Sergeant?"

Fleming laughed. "That's a fair guess," he said, climbing out of his car and stepping on his cigarette before leaning down to look in at her. "It's a beautiful day for almost anything."

She said, "But murder."

He nodded, sensing something was on her mind. "But murder, Miss Maitland. Are you settled in up there on your hilltop?"

She said, "Yes," quite briskly, then looked quizzically at him. "In going through my uncle's papers I found something that might interest you."

Fleming kept looking at her as he said, "I'll be grateful, of course, even though Mister Frederickson might disapprove."

The liquid dark eyes narrowed just a tiny bit. "But we're interested in finding a murderer, aren't we? Not in entangling legalities."

Fleming did something he very rarely ever did; he complimented someone. "I liked you the moment I saw you, Miss Maitland, and in my business a man becomes fairly adept at reading people."

She reddened and looked away. "My uncle offered Mrs Marchant two hundred thousand dollars the week before he was killed." The dark eyes swung back. "I found his notation to that effect, Sergeant."

Fleming stood a moment without speaking, then he sagged a little, not because of this revelation, but because it opened up an entirely fresh avenue at a time when he had been fairly certain he knew why Blassingame had been killed, and by whom. He dropped his gaze for a moment, and stood silent, trying to fit this new piece into the rest of the puzzle without any luck at all.

Elisabeth Maitland, watching, finally said, "If you'll drop round tomorrow, Sergeant, I'll give you the note."

Fleming straightened up as she eased the car into gear. "Thank you very much, I'll be out in the morning." As he watched the shiny little car dart on down towards the exit from Forest Hills he said, "Damnation." Then he got into his own car and also drove towards the exit from Forest Hills.

All the way back to the city he juggled this new bit of information without ever finding a way to make it mesh with what he already knew or suspected, and by the time in late afternoon that he reached Mike Sublette's office he was both troubled and irritable.

Sublette was reading back something he had evidently only very recently written on his desk tablet when Fleming arrived. He studied Fleming's face a moment, then said, "If you need cheering up, maybe I've got something that will do it. About your request a couple of hours back: the Davis-Whiting outfit in Richmond, Virginia, is indeed headed-up by Mrs Marchant's father, Lee Whiting. Davis, who was one of the co-founders, died about ten years ago. The reason he did not go to his son-in-law when his company got into trouble was because Richard Marchant and Whiting are not friendly; haven't been friendly, from what I dug up, for a number of years. Eleanor Whiting Marchant is something else: she appears to be fiercely protective of her father."

Fleming sat down in a slump. "Okay; so she went to Dunning as her father's representative, and Dunning offered to bail Davis-Whiting out, his reason being one of the oldest reasons why a man would do a beautiful woman a favour on earth."

"Is she that pretty?" asked Sublette.

"Beautiful," answered Fleming. "She has a young girl's figure and the face to go with it. Not my type, Mike, and probably not your type, but among the patricians she'd be one of the most desirable women around."

Sublette accepted this and pressed on to the next factor. "Okay; maybe she paid Dunning's price and maybe she didn't. That's not too important, is it? She got the money for her father — then what happened? Her husband found out? If that's it, why the hell did he shoot Blassingame? The guy he should have shot was Dunning."

Fleming said, "*He* didn't shoot anyone. He and his wife were in the city the day Blassingame got hit." Fleming sighed as though in resignation. "I'll tell you who Richard Marchant thinks shot Blassingame — his own father. He tried to alibi the old man to me today, purely as an instinctive reflex — when, if he'd thought a moment, he'd have known I already know where the old man was the day of the killing."

Sublette pondered this a moment, then said, "Okay; let's theorise the old man into a murdering position: he lives there and he's no one's fool, so somehow he knew Dunning had given his daughter-in-law money, and maybe he knew what she had to do to earn it. . . ." Sublette let his words trail off. "Hell; then he should have shot Dunning."

Fleming smiled. "Exactly. Just before I drove in this afternoon Blassingame's niece told me she'd turned up a notation saying her uncle had offered Eleanor Marchant a couple of hundred thousand dollars. She did not say what the offer was made for, and I assume from that the notation did not mention this."

Mike Sublette put his head in his hands and groaned. "I'm lost," he admitted. "Was Blassingame also captivated by the Marchant woman? These guys sure pay one hell of a lot of money for —"

"Blassingame didn't make the offer for that purpose," exclaimed Fleming. "Maybe Dunning did; after seeing him and talking to him, I can believe it. But not Blassingame. He was an altogether different variety of fish."

Sublette suddenly said, "Okay; but would *Richard* Marchant know this? Suppose he saw his wife having an intimate conversation with Blassingame?"

"I just told you, Richard was in the city the day Blassingame was shot."

Sublette said, "He didn't have to do the actual shooting, Paul. A guy with millions can hire a killer every day of the year if he wants one."

"Yeah, of course he can, except for one thing. He's got to be that kind of a man — which Richard Marchant is not." Fleming lit a cigarette and tossed the match into a tray on the desk. "The old man *might* kill, but not the son."

Sublette said, "All right. Then let's get back to the father."

Fleming shook his head and reached for the tablet on the desk. "It's quitting time. Let me take your notes on the Davis-Whiting company home and ready them tonight. In the morning I've got to see Elisabeth Maitland, and maybe after that I'll have you drive down."

"For arrests?" asked Mike, and Fleming rose wearing an enigmatic smile. He did not answer as he folded the piece of tablet paper and pocketed it as he went to the door and walked out.

CHAPTER 11

DIFFERENT KINDS
OF WOMEN

Without knowing what the Davis-Whiting company manufactured, and without even much curiosity on that score, Fleming was satisfied, after evaluating what he now knew about the company that it was a losing proposition. Whether this arose, as he suspected, from a faulty infrastructure — faulty leadership at the top — or whether it arose in part from the declining status of government contractors, did not concern him much either. What *did* concern him was a strong suspicion that one reason why Eleanor Marchant resented having a detective nosing around was that she feared he might turn up something — which he had, in fact, turned up — her husband did not know.

Fleming was fairly certain she had kept her dealings with Clarence Dunning entirely to herself. *But,* as well as he got to know old

Peter Marchant, he was a whole lot less sure the older man had not found out, if not everything his daughter-in-law was up to, then at least enough of it. The question that still defied analysis and logical resolution, however, was why, if the old man had taken a hand, Blassingame and not Dunning had been shot?

On the drive out to the Blassingame estate in the early morning Fleming, the professional, and Fleming, the man, were at odds. He could probably make a fair case against the old man; at least enough of a case to arrest him on suspicion of murder. The reason he shrank from this course was purely emotional and he knew it. He liked old Peter Marchant.

As he wheeled up the Blassingame drive he turned to the possibility that young Marchant knew, or had perhaps inadvertently discovered, what was going on between his wife and Clarence Dunning, which would of course make a triangle murder out of Blassingame's death — except that, again, the infuriated husband would have shot Dunning, not Blassingame.

As he climbed out of the car and stood a moment looking around in the warm sunlight, an errant thought arrived: why in the hell, when people had everything, couldn't they, even then, act differently?

Elisabeth Maitland came round the side of

the house, saw him standing out there, and strolled over as she said, "It's far too beautiful a day, Sergeant, to have the burdens of the world on your shoulders. Would you care for a cup of coffee?"

He smiled at her. "Anything but tea, thank you."

She laughed at him, at his glum expression and his sombre stare. "We have something in common, then. I don't care for tea, either. Come along."

She was wearing a sleeveless sweater and a pair of slacks, and she filled them very admirably. Fleming sighed and averted his eyes as he trooped round towards the back patio with her. There, Mary Larkin appeared as though by magic, and after exchanging a smile with Elisabeth Maitland, went after their coffee. Fleming reflected that he had never seen Mary Larkin smile before.

Elisabeth Maitland picked up a slip of paper and handed it to Fleming. In a man's bold scrawl the note stated in simple words that as of the date at the top of the slip of paper Lamont Blassingame had offered Eleanor Marchant two hundred thousand dollars as an unsecured loan. That was all, except for Lamont Blassingame's signature; no reason for making the offer, no explanation as to how it had come to be made, nothing else.

Fleming looked at the woman seated at the

little metal table. She said, "Keep it, if you'd like. Sit down Sergeant, the coffee will be along in a moment." She smiled. "You know, it's almost sinful for anyone to look as solemn as you do on a morning like this."

He felt his spirit flowering a little under her smile and her chiding, but in justification he answered as he pocketed the slip of paper:

"My line of work knocks out all your illusions every day right at five o'clock. And I've been at it quite a few years."

Their coffee arrived, he returned Mrs Larkin's guarded greeting, and after she had departed he tasted the coffee. It was good. Elisabeth Maitland said, "Why would he have written that note and filed it in his personal folder in the desk of his study, Sergeant?"

Fleming was asking himself the same question and so far had no answer, only a vague and unsupportable suspicion which he would not mention. "Tidy," he told her, making a grin. "Meticulous, perhaps; orderly about things like money."

Elisabeth Maitland stared at Fleming and very slowly shook her head. "I don't think you believe that. The Larkins told me you spent several days around here. You probably know my uncle better than I did; men have an affinity for the doings of other men."

Fleming laughed. "You're sure of that, are you?"

She did not return his smile or laughter. "I'm sure of it. As you've been a detective a long while, I've been a nurse. My trade, too, teaches people something about human nature, Sergeant."

He was willing to concede that. "All right; suppose you tell me why your uncle left the note?"

She dropped her eyes. "I can't. I have no idea. But you are a man as well as a detective. You'll have some idea." She suddenly looked up again. "But you don't talk about things like this, do you?"

He shrugged. "No; not as a general rule. Mrs Larkin makes good coffee, doesn't she?"

They exchanged a look and Elisabeth Maitland's quick, delightful smile came again. "Yes, very good coffee. She's also an outstanding cook and housekeeper, and you are adept at changing the subject when you prefer not to talk about something."

He finished the coffee and swung half-around so he could look over towards the bridle path, which was still largely in shade because the morning was not very far advanced.

Across the path and some distance off was the rolling ridge that led up to Peter Marchant's cottage, invisible from where Fleming sat although he knew where it stood beyond the hilltop.

Elisabeth Maitland said, "I had my first social visitor last evening, Sergeant."

He looked back at her, knowing before she said the name who the caller had been.

"Mister Marchant, the elder."

Fleming nodded. "That's interesting."

She corrected him. "*He* is interesting. I visualised him as he was thirty or forty years ago; strong, direct, quick and perceptive and observant. He's still like that, except that retirement has taken the edge off, I think."

"Why did he call?" asked Fleming, not particularly interested in her assessment of the old man.

The brown eyes widened. "You suggested it. At least that's what he told me. He said you'd told him I would make a good neighbour, or something like that."

Old Peter would have said that to put her at ease, but that's not what had brought him to the Blassingame estate. Fleming sat back and waited.

Mrs Larkin appeared to see if either of them wished more coffee; neither of them did, so Mrs Larkin retreated. When this interruption had resolved itself Elisabeth Maitland leaned on the table looking squarely at Paul Fleming.

"He is such a wonderful old man, Sergeant, and he is also so worried. We talked about my uncle for a while; I got the impression that Mister Marchant and my uncle were not exactly close friends, and yet it was obvious that Mister Marchant respected my uncle."

Fleming thought that, so far, Peter Marchant had been in character.

Elisabeth went on speaking. "He told me a few things about the neighbourhood, a little about the people who live in Forest Hills. It was a nice, relaxed visit until after dark, then he went hiking back towards his hill and I felt sorry because he had to leave." The soft brown eyes darkened with irony. "Father-figure, Sergeant?"

Fleming doubted that. "Probably just a lonely old man, and a newcomer to Forest Hills needing a friend." He stood up. "You'll have other callers, no doubt. I'm not up on patrician etiquette, but it seems to me I read somewhere that it is the obligation of people in a community to call on newcomers."

She also rose from the little table. "I'm afraid I'm not up on protocol either, Sergeant, and I'm also afraid I'm too old by now to develop a new personality. I mean, inheriting all this wealth makes me feel — well — a kind of resentment, because it's going to order my life, isn't it?"

Fleming was not by vocation nor avocation a person likely to offer personal advice, and he did not offer it now. All he said was, "The coffee was very good, and your company was even more so. Thanks for letting me keep the note."

She went round to the car with him without speaking again. Twice she stole sidelong glances at him, and he was aware of it, then, as he jack-knifed down into the car and looked out, she had a very faint frown on her face. He thanked her again and drove away.

On the way towards the Marchant estate he thought how easy, and how pleasant, it would be to cultivate Lamont Blassingame's niece, then he put that out of his mind as he turned up the curving, uphill drive that ended out front of the magnificent fieldstone mansion, just as Eleanor Marchant came forth from the front of the house, saw Fleming, and stopped in her tracks as he alighted and sombrely nodded towards her.

She was gloved and hatted and was carrying a purse, so evidently she had been about to go to the four-car garage when Fleming's arrival had riveted her to the flagstone entry-way outside the recessed, arched front door.

To Fleming she looked like a person wishing to flee but who was held there by something equally as unsettling: great curiosity.

He was affable and relaxed as he strolled over and said, "Good morning. If I'm holding you back I could return later. Perhaps this evening."

The swift passing of a shadow over her lovely face was sufficient answer even before she said, "No, Sergeant, I'm not in any great hurry. You wanted to see me? I thought it might be my husband . . ."

"I'll see him too, after a bit," replied Fleming. "I'd like to ask you just one question: last week when we met, Mrs Marchant, and you had just returned from a horseback ride, I got the impression you had been out on the bridle path. Is that correct, had you been riding out there?"

The very clear blue eyes probed for an opening in Fleming's face and found none. He was standing there courteously awaiting an answer, as solid and blank-faced as a life-sized statue. Without showing it, he was also picking up every radiation she was unconsciously sending out: she was fearful and defensive and guarded, all at the same time, and finally, because she was not at all experienced in anything like this, with a policeman, she took the lame way out.

"What day was that, Sergeant? I ride quite often you see, and since it's for pleasure I don't make much effort to remember exactly where I go."

He deliberately said, "Friday, I think," and he saw at once by the flicker of a frown that she knew it hadn't been Friday — so — she remembered which day it was. Then he said, "We talked for a short while down at the stable. You'll remember that. And you'd just come back from a ride. In fact, your stable-man was leading the horse away when I came down there and spoke to you."

Without enthusiasm she said, "Oh yes; now I remember. Well — yes, I rode south on the path that morning." She offered a womanish little smile. "I think that's south, but I never can remember directions. My husband gets so exasperated at me sometimes for that."

Fleming was not to be diverted. "You rode south on the bridle path, then. You know, Mrs Marchant, that's very interesting." Fleming moved into the shade and sat perched upon a great stone lion that was holding up a low railing beside the front door. "I was on the hill for an hour or so before you came towards the barn, admiring the view down by the bridle path, and I didn't see a single rider come along in all that time."

He saw her wilt. She caught her underlip in her teeth and stared at Fleming as though she were hypnotised. Then she rallied and said, "Maybe that's the day I took the short-cut home, Sergeant."

He smiled quietly. "The short-cut?"

"Well, yes; there's a glade north of the trail, Sergeant. Sometimes I ride back that way instead of staying on the path. In fact, I do this quite often."

Fleming said, "Of course. That would account for my not seeing you." Maybe her sense of direction was faulty, but she had just proved that she knew which direction the glade was in from the bridle path. He stood up. "Thank you. I won't keep you any longer."

She nodded and turned to walk very swiftly in the direction of the garage.

CHAPTER 12

FLEMING'S LITTLE HUNCH

Fleming paced slowly around the side of the manor house thinking that if Mike Sublette were here with him today he would have had him follow Eleanor Marchant. But as he walked out into the open on his way towards the distant cottage and saw the two men standing down there in the shade of the small porch, he forgot about the woman and concentrated now on her husband and father-in-law. They had seen Fleming and were now facing towards him, having ended whatever they had been discussing when he'd come into view.

The younger Marchant suddenly stepped off the porch and started directly towards Fleming in a direct and strong-striding manner. Fleming could sense the open hostility while they were still fifty yards apart. By the time Richard Marchant was close enough to speak, Fleming nodded and said, "Good morning."

Marchant halted, his expression openly antagonistic. Without returning Fleming's greeting he said, "Sergeant, I don't think it's mandatory for people to be hounded by the police."

Fleming was more at home with someone like this than he was with someone as courteous and withdrawn as young Marchant had been before, when they'd met. Without a smile Fleming said, "You are perfectly right, and on the other hand I don't think the taxpayers should have to buy my gas for the long drive down here every day, either, so probably the solution would be for me to serve you with a warrant of arrest and take you into the city for interrogation."

Marchant reddened. "On what charge?"

Fleming was careful here. If he said suspicion of homicide Marchant would rush to the house and call his attorneys. "There doesn't have to be a formal charge, Mister Marchant; I can hold you eight hours for interrogation, providing you're considered an accessory to a major felony." Fleming paused, then loosened a little. "But neither of us want that. All I'd like from you this morning is a little of your time. No more than perhaps fifteen minutes. And I'm sorry if I seem to be coming up here so often. It's not something I like doing, appearing to be hounding people."

"What is it you wish?" asked the younger Marchant, appearing to waver between whatever his earlier resolution had been and a wish to avoid anything as humiliating as Fleming had suggested happening to him.

"I believe the first time we talked," said Fleming, "you told me your only association with Lamont Blassingame was social; is that correct?"

Marchant bobbed his head just once. "Yes."

"And I seem to recall that when we discussed Blassingame in the role of a Casanova you didn't think much of the idea."

Marchant was beginning to show impatience again. "I still don't, Sergeant. Blassingame was a single man; if he'd needed — companionship — he certainly wouldn't have had to risk entanglements in Forest Hills. After all, Los Angeles isn't much of a drive, and there are all kinds of opportunities up there."

Fleming said, "I think you're right. Would there be anyone else around here, in Forest Hills I mean, who might fit the category of a Casanova?"

Richard Marchant scowled. "Are you investigating a case of infidelity, Sergeant, or a murder?"

Fleming said nothing, he stood there looking at the younger Marchant — who had just answered the real question for Fleming: *Richard Marchant did not suspect anything.*

Marchant finally said, "I can't think of anyone who would live up to that, Sergeant. But then, I'm in town several days a week, and things like local gossip don't really interest me very much. No, I can't think of any local philanderers."

Fleming stepped aside. "Thank you. That's really all I wanted to know. And again, I'm sorry for intruding."

Richard Marchant relented a little. "Well, I realise there is a job to be done. It's simply that my father told me a while ago when we were discussing Dunning's purchase of the glade below the hill, that you and he went hiking down there, and it looked to me as though you were coming around, for some particular reason, on the days when I wasn't home. I suppose that was a hasty judgement, though."

Fleming said, "I understand. Thanks again for your time." As Richard Marchant nodded and continued on in the direction of the manor house, Fleming stood gazing after him. Finally, instead of continuing on down towards the cottage where Peter Marchant was still standing on his shaded porch, watching, Fleming turned and walked thoughtfully back towards his car. He got in and drove back down to the main roadway.

There he revved the engine and put through a call to Mike Sublette.

As before, this took time, but when he finally got through he asked Sublette to check out a car from the motor-pool, bring along some tools, two pairs of coveralls, and meet him at the south gate of Forest Hills as soon as he could.

Afterwards, because it was close to noon, Fleming drove out of the community and cruised the commercial area several miles away where a hungry man could find a place to eat.

He had his motive, and he was reasonably certain he also had his murderer, but in dealings with people like those living in Forest Hills, a badge and a frowning silence would not be enough. He would need a whole lot more; he would have to have physical evidence that would stand up in court, and because those people on their exclusive hilltops would be able to hire the best lawyers on the West Coast — in the entire nation, for that matter — Fleming was going to have to spend almost as much time painfully building up his case, as he had already spent in conducting his investigation.

The restaurant where he finally had lunch was in an area someone had tried to keep exclusive, perhaps with some idea in mind of catching Forest Hills trade, but, as usually happened, a host of grubby little businesses were encroaching. Not that Fleming cared; he did not even live within cannon-shot of this part of the county. And since the food was adequate and the price was not too stiff, he ate and thought, and when he was ready to leave he had already put both the neighbourhood and the restaurant out of his mind.

He was beside his car, his mind on a completely separate plane, when a little shiny dark car slid in behind him and its driver touched the horn-button.

Fleming recognised the car even before he sought out the dark-eyed driver who was smiling up at him. He strolled back and leaned down. Elisabeth Maitland said, "I wasn't really following you, or I'd have worn a beard and dark glasses."

He laughed. "I'll buy your lunch."

She slid out of the car and stepped with him to the kerbing. "No, thanks. I wouldn't want you to have to sit through all that when you've obviously just eaten." She looked away, then back again. "But you could buy my *dinner*."

He almost snapped her up, but Mike Sublette was on the way and there was no way of telling how long their joint enter-prise would take. He said, "Tomorrow night?"

She nodded and when he almost asked what time to drop by for her she excused herself and hastened into a near-by store. Not until he was getting into his car did it occur to him that he was going to have to make the long — even *longer* — drive, from his apartment out in Westwood, to her hilltop in Forest Hills. There had been times, lately, when he'd felt more like a taxi-driver than a policeman.

But she was worth it.

He headed back towards the south entrance to Forest Hills, checked his watch and made an estimate that Sublette would be along within the next hour, and drove a little aimlessly up through the residential area in the general direction of the golf club. But he did not stop there.

Where the road curved around a low hill heading slightly south as well as west, he drove past several estates he had seen before but knew nothing about, and not too long afterwards had the distant west gateway in sight. From there, he left Forest Hills by passing between the whitewashed stone pillars that marked each entrance, and turned left, which was straight south.

This roadway carried more traffic, and it was not even a good secondary thoroughfare. He halted, finally, where he encountered the beginning of the bridle path. By now he had a fair idea of the lie of the entire Forest Hills community, at least with respect of the area he was interested in.

By going up the bridle path from where Fleming now was, for perhaps three-quarters of a mile, it would be possible to come to the big curve with the glade to the north, and both the Blassingame and Dunning estates south and east. Otherwise, beyond the curve and on the north-east was the lower paddock, or pasture, of the Marchant estate.

He drove on, making the complete circuit until he was back at the south entrance, and when he had been sitting there for a short while, Mike Sublette arrived. They walked back behind Mike's car to look in the boot. Sublette ticked off the articles packed in there, then he slammed the lid down, dusted his hands and looked ahead towards the nearest hilltop residence, which happened to be the Dunning house.

"Very nice," Mike said, and Fleming grunted as he studied his watch. It would not be nightfall for another four hours at the very least, this being summertime.

Fleming headed for his car. "Follow me," he ordered, and although Sublette had to be mystified, he, too, was a career policeman, so mysteries, even minor ones, did not upset him.

Fleming drove back round to the place on the west side of Forest Hills where they could leave their cars, take their equipment, and start the hike inland by way of the bridle path. Sublette said nothing as they divided the equipment between them, then started up the trail.

It was hot in the places where they had to leave tree-shade, but Fleming's concern was with what they were doing, not on the discomfort. He told Mike to stay to the shade as much as he could, and when he crossed the sunshiny places to do it swiftly. Sublette's comment was plaintive: "You sure this isn't a case for the Canadian Mounted Police?"

Finally, when they were nearing the bend in the trail, and could see the houses on ahead on both sides of them, Fleming halted and lit a cigarette and hooked his arms over the white fence on his right. "The farthest house southward belongs to a man named Dunning. You've run across the name before. The house next on our left is Blassingame's place. That dark patch along the back is a shaded patio. That's where he was sitting when someone shot him. The house on across the path, northward, is the back of the Marchant place, and that cottage closer to us up there belongs to the elder Marchant."

Mike studied the Blassingame place with a perplexed scowl. "You mean someone picked Blassingame off from here when he was sitting up there in the shadows? He'd have to be one hell of a good shot, Paul."

Fleming straightened up. "Not from here.

I think the shot came from another quarter-mile farther along; maybe even closer than that. But the rifleman was a good shot, even then." Fleming dropped his cigarette, stamped it out, picked up his tools and paused for a moment looking towards the Peter Marchant cottage. "I suppose, if we were smart, we'd wait until nightfall to do this."

Sublette, looking up where Fleming was staring, said, "Why? Are you thinking this marksman might see us?"

Fleming said, "Come on, and stay in the shadows. Yeah; I was thinking something like that."

Sublette was a very practical man. "Well, hell," he said in his most practical voice, "let's wait until after dark, then."

But Fleming had considered this much earlier in the day, and for what he had in mind they would need daylight. Even electric torches wouldn't be adequate.

Fleming crossed the path, clambered over the nearest fence, waited to assist Sublette also get across, with all their tools, and finally Fleming began to lose his sense of urgency and wariness. From this point on no one would see them because of the trees, but if they had made this attempt after dark, there was a very good chance that more than one person would have seen *someone* down in the glade shining torches about.

131

Mike Sublette almost fell when he stumbled over a half-concealed tree root, and swore with hearty feeling. Fleming wanted to laugh, but instead he said, "Look where you're going, will you?" and kept right on heading through the trees towards the glade beyond.

CHAPTER 13

AN EXHUMATION

When they eventually halted in the tree-fringe, facing towards the grassy glade beyond, and Mike set aside the things he had been carrying and mopped his face with a handkerchief, he said, "Would you mind telling me just what the hell we are doing here?"

Fleming said, "Looking for a grave," and missed the quick look he got from Mike Sublette. "That's why we have to do this in daylight. And with torches after dark we probably would never find it." Fleming looked at Sublette. "We may not find it now, either." He gestured. "If you'll start walking in a big circle on the edge of the glade up northward, I'll do the same heading around down here, and we'll meet over across the way. Take one of the shovels, Mike, and look closely for any indication that the soil has been disturbed. If you find such a place, shove your shovel in it to be sure someone's dug there. And don't make a lot of noise. I doubt very much that anyone's going to come down here, especially at this time of day, but it's quiet around Forest Hills, and there's an old man living in that cottage up there east of us. He'll sure as hell become curious if he hears noise down in here."

Sublette proceeded to shed his jacket and don one of the denim pairs of coveralls he had brought. Fleming did the same, and just before they parted Sublette said, "Just how sure are you that there's a grave around here?"

Fleming smiled. "Not sure at all. It's a hunch. And until about noon today the idea didn't even occur to me. Someone said something that made me wonder."

Sublette picked up his shovel, flung it across his shoulder as though it were a rifle and said, "Great. I'm going to miss dinner and work overtime because someone said something that got your little wheels turning. Okay; but you owe me a dinner, win or lose." Sublette went off along the edge of the trees, and just before he was cut off from Fleming's view, Fleming saw him slap violently at the back of his neck where a mosquito had landed.

It was hot and still and humid, and putting on the suit of coveralls did not make Fleming feel any cooler. The flimsy reason that had made him undertake this enterprise did not seem as valid now, either, as it had seemed when he'd been talking to Richard Marchant. But Fleming knew how this kind of thing was; a man's suspicions seemed best when he first had them, and afterwards they became less and less reasonable. But there was a saving grace, at least this time: if he and Mike Sublette came up with nothing, only he and Mike Sublette would know.

Failure was usually not a great sin. It was humiliating, but any detective who had worked at his trade for a few years was thoroughly familiar with failures that resulted in humiliation. If Fleming failed in this, but still broke the Blassingame murder assignment, he would be satisfied.

As he made his way very carefully in the general direction of the bridle path, and gradually went on around until he was moving westerly around the lower end of the tree-hidden glade, he kept an intent watch for disturbed earth although he thought it highly unlikely what he sought would be down here. More likely, it would be up where Mike Sublette was exploring.

Later, as Fleming reached the west side and started walking up it, facing north, he noticed that the shadows were beginning to deepen, were beginning to form out a short distance from the trees across the glade. He thought it was probably about five o'clock, which meant they still had plenty of time.

He had almost completed his half-circle and paused to look up ahead for some sign of Sublette, and had found no sign of disturbed ground at all. Of course, one sweep did not cover more than a third of the glade so he was not disappointed. Then he saw Sublette approaching and leaned on his shovel until Mike came down the last fifty feet and shook his head.

"If there's a grave in here," said Sublette, "it's not along the border of the trees and the clearing." Mike pointed out towards the exposed area. "I think even in broad daylight, as secluded as this place is, if I were going to dig a grave I'd do it out there and stay away from the trees where roots would give you a bad time. Suppose we go down to the south end and walk northward up the centre of the clearing with about twenty yards between us. That way we'd be able to cover all the open ground."

Fleming was agreeable although he did not believe what they sought would be out in the open. His reason for thinking this was simply because the murderer of Lamont Blassingame had proved himself to be a very wary individual; someone who looked first for good cover.

Fleming was right. As the shadows continued to lengthen, even though beyond the trees daylight was as bright as ever, Fleming paced northward covering the west half of the glade while Mike Sublette, a number of yards on Fleming's right, paced northward covering the east side, and when they got to the upper end of the glade a half-hour later, after having walked slowly and meticulously the full distance, Sublette threw up his hands.

"Okay, it's your baby," he told Fleming. "I've had my say, and now I'll shut up."

Northward, the trees were sparse enough for observers to be able to see up the far slope beyond. Fleming said, "As long as we're up this far let's poke around towards the sidehill" — and that was where Mike Sublette, on Fleming's right and only perhaps a dozen yards beyond the clearing, suddenly halted, lowered his shovel and without a word plunged it into the ground where dead grass, the only *dead* grass close by, formed a drooping, brown outline. Fleming watched, and as the first shovelful of loose earth was turned up he went over there.

Sublette leaned on his shovel, looking up. "Pretty damned small grave," he said, and pointed to the tan outline. "But this is it."

Sublette was right. They took turns digging, neither of them saying a word. Finally, two feet down in the soft, mouldy earth, Fleming dropped his shovel, got down to his knees and pushed warm soil aside to reveal something wrapped in black plastic.

Sublette grunted at the sight and Fleming moved more dirt with his hands, then leaned farther and lifted out the buried object. Sublette watched him unwrap it, then Sublette said, "A rifle?"

Fleming stood up without speaking, shook off the last of the soil and held the gun up. He was elated without showing it. This was the particular piece of evidence he needed, and he had no doubt at all but that a ballistics test would prove this to be the weapon that had fired the slug into Lamont Blassingame's head. He handed the gun to Sublette, picked up his shovel and pro-ceeded to fill in the hole. While he worked Mike Sublette examined the weapon very gingerly so as not to make an overlay of his own fingerprints, just in case there might be other prints on the steel parts of the gun, and he finally spread out the plastic cover-ing then laid the gun upon it. As he then helped Fleming fill in the hole he said, "That's the first thirty-ought-six I've ever seen fitted with a silencer."

They made the hole as nearly as it was as they could, even to getting down on their knees and replanting the stands of dead grass and patting them into place, then gathering twigs and leaves to spread across the place. "In case," said Fleming, "our mur-derer comes back to make sure everything's as he left it."

138

Dusk was beginning to settle, finally. Fleming was surprised when he looked at his watch; it was seven o'clock. He had not been aware of the passage of time during and after the exhumation.

When he was satisfied he picked up the rifle in its plastic covering and smiled at Sublette. "Okay, now I'll buy you that dinner. Let's get out of here."

Sublette did not move. "Who buried it here?"

"The murderer," replied Fleming. "Who else?"

Sublette slung a shovel over his shoulder, looking acidly at his companion. "Very good deduction, my dear Watson. Now — who the hell *is* the murderer?"

A dog barked north of them and Fleming whirled. Up atop the hill behind was a large, tail-wagging German shepherd. He seemed to have their scent but not their sight. Fleming raised a hand to warn Sublette not to move, and when the dog finally angled along the rim to the east, Fleming started moving over into the westerly fringe of trees.

Sublette, looking back, did not see anyone with the dog and remarked about this, but Fleming was moving faster now, as they got into the covert, and only glanced back once or twice as he hurried down towards the bridle path. They were loaded with equipment, and the rifle wrapped in plastic. When

139

they got to the fence Fleming climbed over first, made certain the trail was unoccupied in both directions, then he jerked his head and Sublette also climbed over.

The dog was somewhere behind them, occasionally barking, but not, Fleming thought, in a menacing manner. Finding them seemed to be a game with him. Mike Sublette, though, looked back often. When they were mid-way back to their cars he said, "Well, here he comes," and Fleming paused in the soft-settling gloom to turn back and watch.

The dog still had not seen them, but he was trotting along, nose on the ground, evidently having no difficulty keeping to their trail. He was a large, handsome animal.

Mike said, "You got any idea how many times I've been bitten since I've been a cop?" and unzipped his coveralls half-way down and reached inside where his shoulder-holster was.

Fleming leaned the rifle and shovel against the fence and walked back a few yards, then whistled. At once the big dog threw up his head. As soon as he saw Fleming he barked and stood back, wagging his tail. Fleming went ahead slowly, talking to the animal. Behind him Mike said, "Come on; there might be someone with him back there."

Fleming got close and bent down. The dog was wary but friendly, and after a long moment of wariness and indecision he went up to Fleming grinning and wagging his tail even harder.

Fleming scratched the dog's back, spoke to him, and in a moment they were close friends. Sublette took his hand away from the concealed gun but did not offer to go back where Fleming was.

Finally, Fleming knelt and felt for the tag on the dog's chain collar. There were two metals tags affixed, but they were both devoid of an owner's name. One was a licence, the other was a record of rabies inoculations. Fleming was certain he had not seen this handsome large animal before. Nor did he believe the dog had a two-legged companion; if there had been someone with him, by now he'd have been calling his dog.

Finally, Fleming stood up, patted the dog's head and went back to retrieve the things he'd leaned upon the fence. "Just a friendly pup out exploring," he said, as Sublette nodded and kept a wary eye on the dog. As the two men resumed their walk the dog stood back, still wagging his tail but making no move to accompany the strangers. The last Mike saw of him was when he and Fleming went round the far curve in the bridle path.

Dusk was mantling the entire countryside much faster by this time, and beyond the trail when it was possible to see that secondary road where they'd left their cars, the distant lights of the city, of traffic, even of several distant avenues, were visible.

They put the wrapped weapon in the back of Fleming's car, deposited their coveralls and digging implements in the boot of Sublette's car, then, as Sublette straightened his jacket and tie and shirt, and while Fleming lit up, something caught Sublette's attention and he pointed.

"Look under the windscreen-wiper of your car, Paul."

It was a piece of heavy paper and although Fleming could not make out the writing on it, he did not have to. It was a traffic citation, put there, evidently, by some passing prowl car.

Sublette could not hold back his laughter. "Illegal parking. You ought to be ashamed of yourself."

Fleming looked over where Sublette's car was parked. There was no citation under his windscreen-wiper. "It's discrimination, pure and simple," he said. They laughed together, then they drove away looking for a place to eat. Digging, under almost any circumstances, helped a man work up an appetite.

By the time they found a place that suited Fleming, who was not exactly a discriminating diner but who avoided cafés with garish lights and dirty windows — his two criteria for bad restaurants — Mike Sublette had been patient long enough. As they sat down in a booth and ordered dinner, he asked Fleming just what in the hell he knew about the Blassingame murder, and Fleming told him, recapitulating up to the moment they had found the buried gun, but not once mentioning the identity of the murderer.

CHAPTER 14

A MATTER OF EVIDENCE

Fleming was disappointed. After waiting around all morning for the laboratory report on the exhumed rifle, despite the fact that the bullet that had killed Lamont Blassingame definitely had come from the rifle, there were no fingerprints excepting one smudged set belonging to Mike Sublette. The weapon, said the report, had been wiped clean prior to burial. Several bits of lint from the wiping rag had been determined to be from a common variety of inexpensive cotton cloth such as would be found in almost any home in the country, either in the form of a dish-towel, a handkerchief, or perhaps even a cheap, grey work-shirt.

Sublette seemed to sense Fleming's disappointment because he said, somewhat encouragingly, "That's not the end of it; they've still got the serial number."

Fleming growled his reply to that. "Sure;

and it'll go back to some World War One arsenal, and through a few dozen sporting-goods stores after that, then it'll die out. I wish to hell Congress would pass a law making gun-registration mandatory."

Sublette shrugged without comment. Of course, that would not help either, because unless such a law had been passed twenty years earlier, there would still be no record of this particular old weapon; not, at least, within the last few years, and that was what Fleming needed.

"No prints," he growled, "no identification of the lousy gun. Sure, I knew it was the murder weapon even before we brought it in, but what good is that without a way to connect it to someone?"

Sublette sifted through some papers on his desk while he waited for Fleming to shake this mood. The telephone rang, Mike picked it up, said his name, then listened a moment and held it out. "For you. It's Peter Marchant."

Fleming hadn't expected anything like this. He took the telephone and said his name. It was a good connection despite the distance and the old man's voice came on strongly as he said, "By any chance are you coming out to Forest Hills today, Sergeant?"

Fleming answered thoughtfully. "This evening. Unless it's something important. Then I could drive out right now."

Marchant said, "This evening will be soon enough. The world isn't going to come to an end between now and then."

As Fleming replaced the instrument upon its cradle and gazed over at Sublette he recounted Marchant's statement verbatim. Sublette was interested. "Every little bit helps. Maybe the old lad's going to cop a plea or something."

Fleming rose to depart. At the door he said, "No chance. If that old man had done it, you could drag him behind wild horses before he'd ever admit it. He's the last of a rare kind."

Fleming spent the morning at the offices of the Securities and Exchange Commission, running queries through their teletype. Like most government offices, the Commission had an immense network of sub-offices all across the nation. The office in Richmond, Virginia, however, being a regional headquarters, was as large as was the regional office for Southern California. It also happened to be much more efficient than most government offices, which pleased Fleming. He got answers to his queries faster than he could have got them in almost any other way excepting perhaps a direct telephonic communication. The reason he did not use the telephone was because he wanted his answers in writing.

That was how he got them. Davis-Whiting Manufacturing Company, his first reply noted, due no doubt to a fresh infusion of capital several months earlier, was now operating at full-scale again, but the same shortcomings which had caused the earlier faltering were still endemic. Those shortcomings, according to the Commission's private analysis, derived from the fact that overheads, meaning mostly salaries at the top, were excessive in comparison to the size of the manufacturing operation, plus the fact that with government defence-spending cut-backs hurting nearly all government-oriented manufacturers, Davis-Whiting had made no concerted attempt to secure other contracts either from the civilian agencies of the government or from such civilian-oriented industries as existed in Detroit, where cars were assembled, or from the major aircraft companies. The Commission said that Davis-Whiting stock, while adequately secured, as required by law, had been declining for several years, and even with fresh capital, since the company was not changing either its policies nor its planning, the current liquid position could only last as long as the new capital lasted.

Fleming, who was not even a novice financier, read all this without more than cursory interest. It was when he got the answer to his second teletype that his interest picked up.

The fresh capital had been traced by the

Commission's Richmond office to the daughter of the President of Davis-Whiting, Mrs Eleanor Whiting Marchant. It was not this item that interested Fleming, though. In the next paragraph the report said that subsequently, eight weeks later, in fact, the Richmond securities exchange recorded that three thousand shares of Davis-Whiting had been purchased on the open market. The purchaser in whose name these shares had been made of record was Peter Marchant.

Fleming's next query concerned all shareholders of record, and that was how he learned that individual shareholders did not necessarily have to list themselves by name; for example, although he found that there were two additional Californians in possession of Davis-Whiting shares, one was listed as Southwest Investment Company and the other was shown merely as Meredith Enterprises.

His last enquiry concerned Lee Whiting himself, and here the Richmond office turned careful. It listed him simply as President of Davis-Whiting, a native Virginian, associated with a number of philanthropic undertakings, and that ended Fleming's teletype communications for the day.

But not his other communications with Richmond. He contacted the Richmond F.B.I. office, on a wild guess, but they knew nothing about Lee Whiting except that he was a pillar of the Richmond social set. The same response came through the Richmond detective bureau.

Evidently, ineptness aside, Eleanor Marchant's father was nothing worse than another individual trying to function out of his depth. The world was full of such people. As long as they stayed within the law, at least in the U.S., no matter how their shareholders suffered as a result of their ineptness, they were not liable to criminal prosecution.

Fleming was satisfied about Lee Whiting. He even thought that it was very probable that Whiting did not have any idea what the real source of his fresh capital was; in all probability, too, he would have been chagrined, to say the least, if he had known how his daughter had managed to get that money.

Fleming went over to the Records Bureaux and left the name of those two California companies, Meredith Enterprises and Southwest Investment Company, to be checked out as to actual location, street address and perhaps suite number, and also because he wanted a full list of the officers of each company, as well as the major financial supporters.

Then he went out to lunch.

Later that afternoon he got on a telephone to make a personal investigation of the Marchants, Richard and Peter. He was almost positive what he would learn, and that was precisely what he *did* learn; they were both so solvent and ethical that not so much as a hint of any kind of scandal or irregularity had ever become attached to either of their names.

He then made the same kind of telephonic investigation of Clarence Dunning, even though he already knew quite a bit about the man, and here the record was a little spotty. Dunning had never actually been in any scrapes with the law, but in *civil* actions he had been through the courts any number of times, and in each instance it had to do with sharp financial practices. Also, he had taken others into court many times, almost invariably because of some kind of financial default.

He wanted to know the details about Lamont Blassingame as well, but he did not bother doing his research about the dead man by telephone. Instead, he went home early, showered, re-shaved, got dressed for his date with Blassingame's niece, and as he headed through the late-day traffic towards Forest Hills he flicked through his inventory of places to take someone to dinner, and finally decided that, as sick and tired of driving back and forth as he was, the best place would be a quiet and expensive supper club he had upon occasion taken other dates to; the fact that it was nearer the city's environs in the same general direction as Forest Hills swayed him.

There was one other person he wanted information about: Eleanor Marchant. That would wait until morning. Another aspect he had thought about but had discarded because he hadn't felt that it was entirely relevant yet, was the military record of the four men he was interested in. As Mike Sublette had said, and as Fleming had observed to himself at the outset of his current assignment, the killer of Lamont Blassingame was no novice with a rifle.

Originally, because of the vintage of the murder weapon, he had leaned a little towards the notion that the killer could have been Peter Marchant, the only person involved who had been alive during the heyday of those old-time World War One rifles. But only a little reflection had convinced him that this was not really a very valid supposition; those old guns had proven so popular, so durable and foolproof, that a great many men who hunted, or who just liked to own rifles, had grown up with a .30-.06 at hand.

Of one thing he was certain: the murderer had known exactly what he was doing when he had chosen his murder-gun. Regardless of what Ballistics turned up about the weapon, any fairly good lawyer could tear it all to shreds when it came down to pinpointing ownership. And regardless of whether Fleming could prove in court that this particular gun was indisputably the weapon from which had been fired the fatal shot, unless Fleming could prove beyond a doubt who had owned the gun at the exact time of the murder, the gun and even the bullet fired from it that had taken Blassingame's life, would be worthless as evidence.

Fingerprints would have resolved that beautifully. But there were no fingerprints.

Fleming turned in at the south gate of Forest Hills, shot a look at the lighted residence atop Dunning's knoll, looked in the opposite direction, which was eastward, and saw other lights atop other knolls, here and there, and decided that Forest Hills, at night, reminded him of a medieval countryside where all the barons and knights had their castles atop hills, where they perched like predators, waiting for something worthwhile to pass through down below so they could pounce upon it. The difference now was that the landed barons did not have to pounce; they could simply sit atop their hills and clip coupons or read their investment summaries, and that, he told himself with a grin as he turned up the Blassingame roadway, sure beat the hell out of being buckled into a hundred-pound suit of plate steel and being boosted into a saddle atop a one-ton horse to lead a charge down from the castle-keep.

There were lights on all along the downstairs section of the Blassingame residence. When Fleming raised the knocker at the front door he could hear music inside. He dropped the knocker, heard its clatter echo beyond, and wondered if Lamont Blassingame had played music in the evenings. Probably not.

Mary Larkin in a starched, pale blue dress with a small white apron, opened the door. She looked so different, so friendly and almost radiant, that Fleming gazed a moment rather owlishly at her before stepping inside.

Elisabeth appeared from the direction of the large dining-room. She too looked different; her coppery hair had been piled high. It shone like old brass in the reflected light from behind her. She was wearing some kind of ear-rings that sparkled in a blue and subdued way. The dress she was wearing had a wide, rather low, square neck. It rounded out over her breasts and followed down the flatness of her middle almost to the hips, then it was fuller. She was beautiful — and Fleming remembered something with a sinking heart: he had meant to stop along the way and buy a dozen long-stemmed American Beauty roses.

CHAPTER 15

A PAIR OF SOCIAL CALLS

Detectives were people whose senses were trained to react to ordinary things in a way that most people quite overlooked, but something short-circuited Fleming's senses while he stood gazing at Elisabeth Maitland. Otherwise he would have noticed the tantalising fragrances coming from beyond the large dining-room. Even when she came forward to greet him, he still did not notice. In fact, not until he told her he had only stopped by to explain that he had another stop to make this evening, and would return in no more than an hour, did he catch the aroma. But by then she was telling him what she had done.

"It's quite all right. Just don't be gone longer than an hour, otherwise the steaks will be ruined." At his solemn contemplation of her, Elisabeth smiled. "Don't be angry. The idea of you having to do all that driving

— out here to pick me up, then back here later to drop me off, then back through town to your apartment after midnight — it just seemed like a terrible imposition. Mary and I made supper, and afterwards we can just sit and relax." Her lovely dark eyes searched his face. "Are you disappointed?"

He said, "You're beautiful. But I've said that before, haven't I?"

She laughed, turned him by the arm and went back out into the balmy night with him to the car. "One hour. If you're any later you'll get boot-leather." She leaned down as he got back behind the wheel. "I should have called you first, I know, but I didn't know where to reach you."

He looked out. With that lighted mansion behind her and the cobalt sky farther back and higher, to augment the background, she seemed more golden and rounded than ever.

"You don't have to call me. Just think of my name and I'll appear." He leaned to punch the starter. "You must have read my mind; I don't get very many home-cooked dinners. And you're right — I'm getting fed up with spending hours on end behind a steering-wheel." He smiled. "By any chance are you a mind-reader?"

Her teeth shone bone-white as she straightened back. "One hour — or boot-leather."

He cruised back down to the main thoroughfare, swung left and drove directly to the Marchant estate. As he swung up the private roadway and dimmed his lights so they would not glare across the front of the house when he got up there, he blew out a big, ragged breath. Odd thing about — well — some women and some bachelors. He'd seen a thousand handsome women, and maybe a hundred or so had smiled back at him, but there hadn't been anything more fulfilling than a chemical reaction. Now, in something like two days, even when he was engrossed with something like a ballistics report on a murder rifle, simply by letting his eyes wander from the printed page he could visualise a smiling, dark-eyed woman with dark copper hair, without even being aware that he was thinking about her.

He stopped in front cf the Marchant residence, debated briefly whether or not to tell the younger Marchants he had come in response to a summons from the elder Marchant, decided not to bother, and went hiking on around the south side of the house towards the cottage out back.

Peter Marchant's cottage was lighted throughout, even the small front porch had an overhead light on, as though Fleming might lose his way and would need a beacon. When he got back there and raised his hand to knock, the door opened and the older man, in a loose-fitting smock-like grey shirt of rough material, smiled and beckoned him inside.

"Beautiful night," he said to Fleming, gazing at Fleming's jacket and trousers as though he had never seen a detective dressed for a date before, which in all probability he hadn't. "This really could have waited, Sergeant. It's nothing earth-shattering. Please be seated."

Fleming sat, and through the west-wall picture window saw the sweep of starry sky beyond, and lower, down along the rim of the world, the hazy brilliance of city lights.

Marchant said, "Coffee?"

Fleming declined, and stole a glance at his wristwatch. The older man sank into a large chair and offered a craggy smile. "I suppose I should have done this last week." He made a little gesture as though to wave that away, or as though he might be tired. "There are always things a man doesn't like to think about, let along talk about."

Fleming started to reach for a cigarette, then remembered old Marchant's aversion and let the hand drop back to the arm of the chair.

"I'll start at the beginning, Sergeant, and you can stop me when you have to." Marchant crossed one gaunt leg over the other one, glanced briefly at a photograph of a pleasant-faced woman with snow-white hair which was atop a stereo set near where

Fleming was sitting, then said, "You asked once — at at least you implied, once — that in my ambles round the countryside I might have seen things. Well, my son doesn't know this, I'm quite positive, but twice I saw my daughter-in-law meet a man down below where the bridle trail makes that big turn towards the south-west." The steady grey eyes flicked back to Fleming. "You know the place?"

Fleming knew it, so he nodded.

"I thought you would, Sergeant. Well, the first time I was hiking along the north hillsides and only saw them from a distance, and didn't really think anything about it. She rides quite a bit, you know."

Fleming had a question. "Was the man also riding?"

Marchant said, "No; he was on foot. I assumed he'd been out hiking exactly as I was."

"Who was he?"

Marchant shrugged. "That time, I wasn't sure. They were talking in the shade, and I was too far away. I recognized Eleanor and the horse, but the man was not identifiable from where I was. Actually, I only paused — that time. After all, as I said, she rides a lot, and you can usually run across someone out here if you're out of doors on a warm day. But about a week later I saw them again at the same place."

"The same man?" asked Fleming, and Marchant nodded.

"The same man in the same tweed jacket, thin, grey hair, stocky build."

Fleming sat up a little straighter. "Thin grey hair?"

Marchant paused. "Yes. Thin grey hair, stocky build. This second time was over near the glade, so I did the unpardonable; I slipped over through the trees to get a better look. He was in the shade again, but I was much closer. It was Lamont Blassingame."

Fleming felt nothing, so his face showed nothing. He thought he knew why Blassingame had met with old Marchant's daughter-in-law, and the date of Blassingame's note about the offer to loan Eleanor Marchant that money coincided in a general way with the time Peter Marchant had seen the two people meeting on the bridle path. If it became important, later on, he could pin Marchant down to a specific date, but right at the moment Fleming was not that interested.

Peter Marchant started speaking again. "I did nothing, of course. It could have been coincidental, even that second time . . . Then someone killed Monty, and they shot him not very far from where Eleanor had been meeting him."

Fleming said, "Mister Marchant, specifically, what do you have in mind? That your son may have known of these meetings?"

The old man let his gaze drift to the picture atop the stereo cabinet again before speaking. "I don't know. I simply know that Eleanor was meeting Blassingame. If it wasn't a casual meeting, why didn't he come here, or why didn't she — and Richard — go over there?"

Fleming glanced at his watch again. He had a half-hour yet. He said, "There's something that intrigues me a hell of a lot more, Mister Marchant. The three thousand shares of Davis-Whiting stock you bought a short while back."

The old man's face blanked over in surprise. He stared a moment, then he said, "I never sold you short, Sergeant, but you're even more thorough than I expected." When Fleming sat silently, gazing across at the old man, Marchant finally said, "All right. I did that because Lee Whiting, my daughter-in-law's father, is an incompetent damned fool; one of those elegant Southern gentlemen with all the charm in the world, and not a lick of damned sense in his head. He was going under."

"She told you that?"

"Hell no, the *Wall Street Journal* and the stockmarket listings told me that."

"But why did you bail him out?"

Marchant's brows dropped a notch. "Because if he went belly-up, my daughter-in-law was going to be all emotional, and neither her husband nor I want that to happen."

Fleming said, "Does your son know you bought that stock?"

"No. He and Lee Whiting are not the best of friends. My son considers his wife's father to be a nincompoop; one step ahead of being a confidence man — which is a very good estimate of Whiting. And if you're wondering why I didn't let Dick pick up the shares, it was simply because although he'd have done it to keep the old fool solvent, it would've caused a pretty bad situation between my son and his wife — wouldn't it, Sergeant? Me, I don't matter, and if I want to waste my money, that's my business. You see?"

Fleming did not answer the question, he instead asked a question of his own. "By any chance do you operate under a dummy corporation — either as Southwest Investment Company or Meredith Enterprises?"

Marchant stared. "I never heard of either of them. No, I've never operated under dummy corporations, even when it was advisable for tax purposes to do that. I suppose I've been cursed with old-fashioned ethics, Sergeant, but that kind of thing, good business though it may be, always left a bad taste in my mouth."

161

Fleming rose. He had fifteen minutes to get back to the Blassingame residence. "How much of this have you told your son?" he asked, edging towards the door.

Marchant unwound up to his feet. "None of it. But it'll come out now, won't it?"

Fleming said, "It would have anyway, sooner or later. If Whiting is always going to need someone to pump money into his company, eventually your son will probably have the bite put on him, then he'll discover who owns three thousand shares, won't he?"

Marchant shrugged. "Yes, I suppose so." He went out on to the little porch with Fleming and stood there, gaunt and stooped, with both hands thrust deep into trouser pockets. "The shares and the money don't worry me very much, Sergeant."

Fleming understood, so he said, "I don't believe your son knows that his wife was meeting anyone, Mister Marchant. There is one thing you could tell me that I'd like to know: were either you or Richard in the army, by any chance?"

Marchant looked around, obviously puzzled. "He was, during the Korean War, and I was, in World War One. What of it?"

"Whoever shot Blassingame had to be a pretty fair shot."

Marchant said, "My eyesight isn't that good any more, Sergeant."

Fleming said, "Your son . . . ?"

"You know the answer to that; he wasn't in Forest Hills the day Monty was killed."

Fleming said, "That's an alibi, Mister Marchant. He could have been sitting in his car a mile from Forest Hills waiting for the time to walk up the bridle path, take aim and fire. What I'd like to know is how good a shot he was in the army?"

"He didn't qualify as a marksman, Sergeant, and to my knowledge he hasn't fired a weapon since he got out; you know as well as I do that no matter how good you were ten or twenty years ago, if you haven't practised since, you're no better than a rank amateur."

Fleming said, "Yeah, and I also know something else: your son didn't shoot Blassingame. Well, I've got to be getting along." He stood a moment exchanging a stare with old Marchant, then he smiled. "Forget we had this visit. Say nothing about it to your son or daughter-in-law, and if they saw my car out front, cook up a convincing lie. Okay?"

Marchant said, "Okay. Thanks for coming by."

Fleming struck out at a brisk pace to get round to his car; he had exactly six minutes to return to the Blassingame place and because he did not like well-done steak he made haste all the way.

163

CHAPTER 16

THE INTERLUDE

Elisabeth met him just beyond the door and confessed she had been watching for his car-lights. She had probably seen from which direction he had come, and she may even have been able to see the moving headlamps all the way down Marchant's hill to the roadway, but she said nothing about this. She seemed determined not to have his vocation, or anything related to it, interfere with her plans for the evening.

She took him to her late uncle's study where two iced drinks sat upon a tray, and handed him one. It was a very dry martini. He made it last because by habit and inclination he was not much of a drinking man.

He looked around the beautiful room and said, "The first time I was ever in here it put me in mind of some very old monastery, or possibly the meeting place of medieval lords and belted knights." He grinned. "That's pretty wild, isn't it?"

She studied him. "Sergeant, I really believe you are at heart a romanticist. You are a deceptive person. Did you know that?"

He didn't *know* it, but he'd *heard* it often enough. "What I really am, Elisabeth, is a frustrated bartender." At her changed expression he said, "Maybe I should have said I'm a frustrated father-confessor. I am fascinated by people — all kinds of people. I want to know their reasons and purposes and motives. Maybe being a detective is some kind of subconscious urge towards compensation."

She finished her drink and waited for him to finish his. Somewhere beyond the room, he heard Mark Larkin at work between the pantry and the dining-room. Everything around him contributed to an atmosphere of calm, safe affluence.

He said, gazing quietly at the handsome large desk and the bookshelves, "Have you ever noticed that people leave something of themselves behind? Your uncle's personality or character, something of him, is still in this room." He faced her. She was still studying him, so he winked roguishly. "Would you believe I get this way after only one martini?"

She smiled. "I would believe you are a very unusual man, Sergeant."

He said, "Sergeant by day. Paul Fleming by night."

"Would you care to have that martini freshened up — Paul?"

The drink was two-thirds gone and, although he did not really feel much need for a re-fill, he acceded and handed her the glass. As their hands touched she said, "Wait here — and if my uncle appears ask him to wait, too?" She swung out of the room and as he watched her leave he wondered, again, but now in a detached manner, why anyone like Elisabeth Maitland would want to be a nurse in Asia; what he had expected had been someone rather tall and thin-lipped, juiceless and sinewy and ascetic. None of that fitted her.

He strolled to the fireplace and stood looking at the exceptionally good oil portrait of her uncle hanging above the mantel, but it was a younger Lamont Blassingame, and although he had never met the man, in life, he did not believe that when Blassingame had died his eyes, his facial expression, could have been quite as pensively thoughtful as they appeared in the portrait.

He was still looking at the portrait when she returned. As she came up beside him and offered the glass, she said, "That's how I always thought of him. He looked about like that when I was a young girl. I suppose because first impressions are most enduring, I've always remembered him like that." She raised her face to the portrait.

Fleming watched her profile. There was a clearly-defined distinction between her jaw and throat, a clean, sweeping line that fell in full rhythmic roundness to her shoulders, and lower, to the heavy, thrusting breasts. Fleming wondered, if he had been a painter, could he have caught that distinctiveness. She turned slowly, drawn half around by his thoughts. He at once lifted the glass and sipped, and because there was less tartness this time he knew she had made his second martini weaker than the first.

The mood was broken.

She went over to a leather chair, sat and put her glass aside. "I got quite a surprise today," she told him in a very conversational manner, as though they were old friends, or at least long-time associates. "I saw Eleanor Marchant." The dark eyes lingered on his face with a soft brilliance. "If you are wondering why it was such a surprise, Paul, go look at the little picture on the shelf at the far end of the bookshelf behind you."

He went, found the portrait in its gold-scroll oval frame, looked a long time, and finally sighed as he turned back. "Who is she?"

Elisabeth said, "My aunt. But she was in her late twenties when that was painted. Did you ever see two unrelated people who looked so much alike?"

He hadn't. Lamont Blassingame's late wife

looked enough like Eleanor Whiting Marchant to be her sister, and while he had been looking at the picture it occurred to him why her uncle had made that no-strings-attached offer of money to Eleanor. What he wondered now was whether her uncle had ever mentioned this to Eleanor. If he had known Blassingame better he probably could have answered that. But even so, he thought he knew enough about the man, even after he had died, to make a fair guess: Lamont Blassingame had *not* told Eleanor.

Without warning Elisabeth said, "Do you suppose it could have been her jealous husband, Paul . . . ?"

He smiled and said nothing as he strolled back to the area in front of the fireplace. He had come to the conclusion long ago that when men were seen primarily as symbols of their occupation, that people just naturally, or perhaps subconsciously, did not differentiate; a doctor was seen less as a human being than as something representative of medicine, a lawyer made people think of their troubles, and a detective reminded people of their personal entanglements which, in Elisabeth Maitland's case, meant the murder of her uncle.

Perhaps she caught some of this, as he stood there thinking it, because she suddenly got up to her feet and said, "I'm sorry.

I didn't mean to let this happen. Not to-night."

Mary Larkin appeared to announce dinner, and that at least was a matter of good timing. They left their drinks and went to the study doorway. There she laid a hand lightly on his arm and looked upwards.

"I won't mention it again."

He felt a strong compulsion; he was acutely aware of her nearness and of her magnetism. He said, "Tell me something, Elisabeth: why a nurse, and why, of all things, a nurse in Asia?"

She understood. "It doesn't fit, does it? Well, the best answer I can give, Paul, is that after ten years — between age twenty and age thirty — I gave up looking." She held his arm and started him moving across towards the distant dining-room. "Sometimes I felt like someone's wise old grandmother, and that's no way to feel at all when you're out with a handsome man, is it? But I always had this sensation of having met him before, of knowing exactly what he was going to say, what he was going to do. And I could see what lay beyond." She stopped and smiled upwards. "A misfit at twenty in a conforming society isn't an altogether happy woman." She tugged him onward again. "So — nursing appealed to me. As for Asia; there was no real reason except that I had to find a place where I couldn't close my eyes and see

169

tomorrow and the day after exactly as they would be. Does this sound a little insane?"

He didn't think so, and he didn't think having her walking beside him this close was like anything he had experienced before, either. Of course, chemistry had a lot to do with it, she was a very striking and voluptuous woman, and he had been without a woman a long while, but that was perhaps less than half of what he felt. The rest of it he would have needed more time to analyse, and as they walked into the dining-room with its gleaming silver and soft candlelight, he was distracted.

The Blassingame dining-room was almost feudal, and again there was that atmosphere of solid strength and unalterable security. Fleming finally discovered why he kept thinking in terms of medieval times, while he was here.

It was not because there was any visible similarity, but the atmosphere was the same. Instead of being behind immensely thick walls and battlemented towers, he was surrounded by the kind of great wealth that inevitably meant power as well as security; the medieval walls had yielded to the same sense of safety that wealth ensured in the twentieth century.

He held Elisabeth's chair, then went along to his own seat. It was really quite easy to fit into this atmosphere, even though

Fleming had never experienced this identical environment before. He smiled to himself: maybe in another life he had been here. Elisabeth caught the shadow of his smile and said, "What is it?"

"Strange thoughts," he said, and turned the subject. "Will you return to Asia?"

She smiled as Mary Larkin came to serve them. "How can I? It's not quite the same as inheriting an attic full of old trunks, is it? Maybe, someday, but Asia won't be the same and, by then, neither will I." As Mary Larkin went soundlessly back in the direction of the pantry, Elisabeth's gaze drifted from Fleming to the silver on display behind the glass fronts along the mahogany-panelled far wall. Overhead, a brass chandelier coloured her darker, made her hair almost rusty black and her smooth face gypsy-like.

"That's what I meant the other day when I told you I almost resented the inheritance. It forces me to change."

He ate a moment, found the steak medium-rare, exactly as he'd have wished for it to be if anyone had asked him, then he said, "You would have changed in any case, Elisabeth. People do that constantly, the same way they shed skin and grow new hair, alter perspectives. You couldn't have remained a selfless nurse in the Orient — or anywhere else — for ever." He gave her a sardonic smile. "If a person has to change, I can't imagine a more comfortable way to do it than by inheriting a fortune."

She laughed. "You're part cynic, part romanticist. I didn't think those things could ever be combined in one person."

The meal was as superb as he would have expected, if he'd thought about it all prior to sitting at the table with her.

For a while they did not talk very much, but when their coffee arrived and Mary Larkin went back for their dessert, Fleming sighed. If he ate like this every night within a year he'd need a hoist to get up from the table after supper. Mary Larkin set an ashtray beside Fleming's coffee-cup and left the room again. He lit up, blew smoke, and let his gaze drift round the handsome room and eventually settle upon the handsome woman near-by. It would be so easy, now, under these almost magic circumstances, to empty out his heart to her. She was looking at him, perhaps waiting. She was certainly not aloof nor distant.

He said, "Buckling on my harness again tomorrow is going to be difficult," and smiled at her. "When the clock strikes twelve I turn back into a detective."

Her eyes were stone-steady and very dark as she said, "But it hasn't struck twelve yet, has it?"

A little later she took him out back through the large sitting-room, to the same verandah where her uncle had died, but neither of them considered that in more than a passing way, because it was a bland, pleasant interlude with a soft-scented night on all sides that belonged exclusively to them.

He killed the cigarette, took down a great lungful of night air and let it out slowly. There were a few lights westerly from the back of the house. Neither of the estates on either side of them, Dunning's place nor the Marchant place, was visible except as rolling dark countryside, so the effect was almost of being entirely cut off and alone, thrown upon their individual resources, as it were.

She turned as easily as though nothing more natural were possible, and he met her half-way, his arms rising. She reached high with both arms to encompass his head from behind and he lowered his face to her.

It was a little as though they were practis ing this art, not indulging in it for the first time, spontaneously. She had subdued fire and a need, while Fleming's hunger was stronger without being demanding, but after a moment he could feel himself being absorbed by her, becoming an equal part of something of which she was also an equal part, which was a sensation he had never before experienced.

The whole world dropped away, sight, sound, and motion. All that remained was the place where they stood, and each other.

CHAPTER 17

A FLEMING-SUBLETTE CONFERENCE

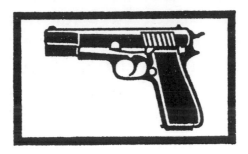

Mike Sublette's patience could, if there was a good enough reason, be almost endless, but when he could see no reason for checking up his irritation, he could and quite often did, become explosive. As now when he glared and said, "Gawddammit, Paul, kick it, will you? This is like talking to a blank wall." Sublette shook some papers across the desk at Fleming. "Look; all that's known about the rifle. And here, Captain McLeod's enquiry, which has to be answered no later than tomorrow." Sublette considered the third paper with an expression of disgust. "Frederickson, Martin and Bishop — that sounds like some rock singing group — Frederickson, Martin and Bishop request information from us before going ahead with the probate procedures of Blassingame's will; they're afraid to do anything until we assure them we are not considering criminal proceedings against Elisabeth Maitland."

Fleming's eyes swung. "Elisabeth . . . ?"

Sublette slowly put the papers upon the desk in front of him without taking his eyes off Fleming. Then he cleared his throat and said, "I don't believe it. I simply do not believe it." He sat back and rolled his eyes upwards as though in supplication before speaking again. "You arrive late this morning, the first time I've ever known you to do that. Then you sit over there like some addict who is bombed out of his mind, a regular damned zombie, until I mention the Maitland woman." Sublette rocked forward again, and leaned with both elbows atop the desk. "How come you arrived late this morning, Paul?"

Fleming reached for the papers and Sublette slammed a big palm down across the same papers. "How come you to walk in here an hour late this morning?"

Fleming answered without raising his head. "I got in late last night."

Sublette nodded fiercely. "Yeah. I believe that. Would you like me to tell you where I think you spent most of the night — and along with that, would you like me to remind you of a regulation concerning personal involvement?"

Fleming's head came up slowly and his mouth was pulled flat to match the toughness of his stare. In a mild tone he said,

175

"Mike, I know you too well to believe you'd ever make a very good chaplain. So forget it, will you? And she is *not* involved."

"She's the victim's niece, isn't she?"

"Yeah. And she was something like six thousand miles away when he got hit. She didn't hire it done, and you can't blow a guy's head open by air mail — yet. Now forget it, will you?"

Sublette loosened his hold on the papers, and Fleming slid them out from under his hand, sat back to light a cigarette and read them. It wasn't easy; last night had been one of those things that, without anyone really anticipating anything spectacular, had burned a vivid memory in Fleming's con- sciousness that nothing could ever exorcise, as though it had all been very painstakingly planned.

Sublette shuffled through the papers on the desk and tossed a folded, crisp paper across. "The blank warrant. A John Doe authorisation for an arrest. You fill it in."

Fleming nodded without taking his eyes off what he was reading. In fact, he did not look at Sublette again until he tossed the papers back on the desk, and even then, although he looked at Mike, he acted as though he had not heard any mention of the warrant.

"Some of the things we had to leave out the last time we kicked this case around are available to us now," he said, and leaned back after punching out his cigarette. "Do you want to take it from the top?"

Sublette nodded his head, but he did not act very enthusiastic.

"Eleanor," said Fleming, "was approached by her father, probably with some thought in mind that she could wring a quarter or a half million dollars out of her husband to keep Davis-Whiting afloat. Her father knew what luck he would have if he flew out here and tried to talk Richard into bailing him out. Maybe it wasn't very chivalrous; not in the best traditions of the Old South, and all that, but when a guy's sinking in quicksand I suppose he's not likely to remember chivalry, is he?"

Sublette sat like stone and said nothing.

"But Eleanor knew she would not only fail with her husband, who held her father in contempt, but that she would also jeopardise her marriage if she insisted. Still, Eleanor was a dutiful or loving daughter, one or the other so she tried to find an alternative."

"She found it," muttered Sublette.

"Yeah, she found it," Fleming agreed. "She dropped a hint in three separate directions. Maybe even *four* directions: her father-in-law's direction, Blassingame's direction, and Dunning's direction."

"Who's the fourth one?" asked Sublette. "Her husband?"

Fleming thought so. "Probably. But just a hint, because she was certain he'd give the idea the cold-shoulder. And he did. So, I'm sure, did Blassingame and her father-in-law. But Clarence, whose business is snapping up any flounders who fall into the shark tank, didn't turn her down. But it wasn't altogether business with him either. He's a wavy-haired, tanned and golden man of the world with a cold bed."

Sublette looked cynical as he said, "Not *that* cold. After he gave her the money for Whiting, he also moved in and started scooping up Davis-Whiting shares."

Fleming's wide mouth drew faintly upwards in an unpleasant small smile. "Yeah. He couldn't resist the temptation. Or maybe, by that time, he'd already had as much of Eleanor as he needed or wanted. But she probably still does not know Dunning was buying shares — someone else knew, though; simply by watching the shares exchange her father-in-law saw that someone was buying in. He doesn't know right now who that is. I know, because I talked to him last night, and if he'd known he'd have told me.

"Anyway, old Peter started picking up shares too. His reason was to block whoever the other buyer was from getting into a position to gain control of Davis-Whiting Manufacturing Company."

Sublette said, "The murder — remember . . . ?"

Fleming laughed. "I'm not forgetting. What we had up until the time of the murder was Dunning having an affair with Eleanor, in exchange for his promise to bail her father out. Which he did by giving her the money, which she sent to her father. Okay; so much for that phase. Now, enter Lamont Blassingame. Tardy, but finally willing to give her a small fortune, too. Only she didn't need it then, did she? The reason Blassingame made the offer was twofold. One, somehow or other he knew she was having an affair with Dunning. Two, she is a dead ringer for his dead wife when Mrs Blassingame was the same age, and that bothered hell out of Blassingame."

Sublette's slouch lessened. He was beginning to learn things, finally. "If this look-alike angle is correct, Paul, then he may have chewed her out for fooling around with Dunning. Right?"

Fleming had arrived at this opinion the previous evening while standing in the Blassingame study gazing at the small portrait of Blassingame's late wife. "I think that's a fair supposition," he told Sublette. "He met her several times — and her father-in-law saw them meet."

Sublette's eyes narrowed. "The hell he did."

"Twice," stated Fleming. "And old Peter's nobody's fool."

"So he shot Blassingame?"

"Wait a minute, will you? Peter thought it over and decided Blassingame and his daughter-in-law were in cahoots to bail out her father. He has never told me this, but I'm sure that either by something he said to her, or perhaps because she saw him spying on her when she was out riding, that she knew he suspected something."

Sublette said, "That made two who knew. Old Marchant and Blassingame. How about her husband?"

"Richard's mind doesn't run to suspicions," Fleming retorted. "But he could have also seen them meeting. You can't live on a hilltop overlooking the countryside and not see people riding the bridle trail below you. But if Richard saw anything, it was his wife with Blassingame."

"So *maybe* he shot him," stated Sublette.

"Maybe. Only he didn't. I think what happened was that either Blassingame, full of rough indignation, went over and told Dunning to break it off, or else Blassingame told Eleanor that he knew of her affair with Dunning, and maybe *she* told Dunning."

Mike scratched the tip of his nose. "Which one, Eleanor or Dunning, hit old Blassingame?"

"That boils down to which one would be in

a position to locate a rifle that could not be traced back to them, and which one was that good a marksman."

Without a moment's hesitation Mike said, "Dunning. No social butterfly I've ever run across could have nailed a guy through the head under those conditions at that distance."

Fleming shrugged heavy shoulders. "Do you know what a high-powered defence lawyer would do to a statement like that in court?"

Sublette knew. "We're not in court, and that's up to prosecuting attorney's office. We're only the investigating officers."

"Like hell," said Fleming, pleasantly. "We're the guys who have to deliver all the evidence to the prosecuting attorney so that he can get a sound conviction for murder."

Mike Sublette left his desk and went over to a window, set his thick back to it and stared at Fleming. "What's the answer; Eleanor?"

Fleming nodded his head. "We're not going to get anything from the strong links in the chain, only from the weakest link. Eleanor."

"How?"

Fleming had no answer to that. "I don't know. And to tell you the plain truth I'm not very enthusiastic. She's going to end up losing a hell of a lot more than she probably ever even imagined was at stake. I've never turned up a murderer that I liked, but I've turned up a lot of indirect accessories that I afterwards saw in my sleep. And there's old Peter Marchant."

Sublette said, "Cut it out. You knew better than to get personally involved before you ever went down there."

Fleming smiled. "Mike, how many times have you sat down to dinner after filing a case, and sat there without any appetite?"

Sublette did not answer. He said, "Get back to Dunning."

Fleming was agreeable. "Okay. Unless he'll tell us before a notary that he owned that damned old rifle — which he'd never do in this world — we have absolutely nothing; not even enough to use as the basis for an arrest on suspicion of murder. So — for the time being we have to leave him out of it. And there is where we're on mighty unsteady ground, because the minute I have a talk with Eleanor to try and get her to take down her hair, she's going to retire to her private boudoir, pick up the telephone, and tell Clarence Dunning we're just about ready to grab him."

Sublette scratched the tip of his nose again. "A guy like that doesn't run. No one with a couple of million dollars ever runs. Just the same, suppose, when you go out to have your talk with Eleanor, I trail after you and keep him under surveillance with a pair of binoculars, and if he *does* get cute, I'll nail him."

Fleming rose and stretched, then he yawned, and a swift look of annoyance passed across Sublette's face. Fleming glanced at his wrist. It was not quite eleven o'clock in the morning. He dropped both arms and looked across towards the far window, which was being almost completely blocked by Mike Sublette. "One word of caution, Mike: this guy is as suave and self assured as anyone you ever saw. And he also happens to have ice-water for blood. You just turn your head once, after he's aware that we're making a case against him, and you could wind up like Blassingame."

Sublette said, "No way, Paul. Absolutely no way under the sun. But it *could* work the other way around, if he puts a hand under his jacket for a handkerchief. Are you ready to go?"

Fleming wasn't ready to go; at least, he did not want to go through with this part of it, but then he seldom enjoyed leaning on an accessory even when the crime was murder. But he went, and on the drive towards Forest Hills he did not have to think of his reason for going out there. He had something else to think about that was much more warming and pleasant.

CHAPTER 18

A FATEFUL MEETING

In the kind of situation Fleming was now in there were a number of variations of two basic options open to him. What it boiled down to was that Fleming could arrest Eleanor Marchant on suspicion of being an accessory to a felony — murder — or he could conduct the interrogation as he was now planning to do, by interrogating her without preferring charges until after he had talked to her, and then making an arrest only if what she told him implicated her — providing she told him anything at all.

On the drive to Forest Hills he wished there were a diplomatic way to do this. The moment he told them at the big house why he was there, Richard Marchant, and maybe even old Peter as well, would insist on being with Eleanor. The revelation that Eleanor had been having an affair would not stun Eleanor's father-in-law, even though he thought her lover was Blassingame not Dunning, but it most certainly would stagger her husband.

Fleming had made a number of untidy arrests in his years as a policeman, and the kind he preferred were those involving physical violence. This other kind, just standing there watching people shrivel under his words, was the worst kind of punishment for Fleming.

When they finally arrived at the stone pillars on either side of the south entranceway to Forest Hills, Sublette wig-wagged with his arm out a window and Fleming slowed, then stopped altogether, got out and walked back.

Sublette pointed to a stretch of bridle path that meandered over a low land-swell heading south-west, then he shoved a pair of binoculars at Fleming. "That's your lady," he said.

Sublette was right. Fleming could see her well enough to make a positive identification. She was wearing a pair of pale jodhpur trousers and a white sweater. Her hair was pulled back on both sides and hung down to her shoulders at the back. She was riding slowly, at a lazy walk, and her slumped posture indicated that the morning sunlight and warmth had made her drowsy.

Fleming handed back the binoculars, plotted her rate of progress along with the direction in which she was riding, and decided to try and intercept her. The meeting would still be bad enough, but at least it would be up to her what she told her husband afterwards, and perhaps a woman could handle something like that better than a man.

Fleming told Mike Sublette what he was going to do, then he said, "There's a chance she might be riding towards a meeting with Dunning. I get the feeling she isn't, but let's be sure. Find a telephone and call him, make sure he's home. If he isn't, find out where he is."

Mike was nodding. "And if he isn't home, I'll duck down along the bridle trail in case you need me." Sublette placed the binoculars carefully upon the seat beside him. As he looked up he said, "Do you have a transceiver in your jockey-box?"

Fleming did have. As he finished watching Eleanor Marchant and started back towards his own car he said, "If he's not out hiking or perhaps riding, keep out of my end of it and concentrate on locating him. Good luck."

The route Fleming took was back out the entranceway and north-west on around the secondary roadway that skirted Forest Hills. His destination was that identical place where he and Mike had left their cars on their digging expedition, and although he had quite a little distance to traverse, his car was a good bit swifter than her horse, so he still expected to be able to intercept her somewhere up the trail, perhaps not very far from the place her father-in-law had seen her meet Lamont Blassingame.

This time, when he parked his car, he pulled it farther away from the secondary road. He still had the traffic citation in his pocket from the previous parking incident at this place.

He thought of taking the two-way radio with him, then decided against it and struck out up the bridle path through humid shade and occasional patches of brilliant sunshine. A hundred yards onward and he was perspiring. Two hundred yards and he had yanked loose his tie and had unbuttoned his collar.

He knew the trail, he knew about how fast — or slow — Eleanor Marchant was riding, and he could estimate just about where he would encounter her. When he was within sight of that big curve where Peter Marchant had seen her speaking with Lamont Blassingame, Fleming stepped to the side of the trail, settling himself comfortably in the pleasant shade of several great oaks and a pair of taller, fairer sycamore trees, lit a smoke and stood lazily relaxed and waiting. By his calculations she should be along within a few minutes.

He was correct. When she came riding

round the curve without seeing Fleming for a dozen or so yards, he recognised the adequacy of his tree-shade camouflage, while at the same time he watched her.

She was a fair woman, and when she wore light clothing she seemed even more fair and golden. Without much doubt, any man, but particularly a wealthy one who was conscious of power and status, would swell with pride when he escorted a woman like Eleanor Whiting Marchant into a room.

Fleming dropped his cigarette, ground it under his heel, sighed and leaned on the white board fence at his back, waiting.

The horse saw him first, and flung up its head. It had been moping along, eyes half-closed, until he'd moved, then it had spotted him at once. It was the horse's reaction that alerted Eleanor Marchant. When she saw Fleming, and of course recognised him, she instinctively lifted her rein hand to halt the horse. She was no more than forty feet away when she did that.

Fleming nodded gravely and strolled a little closer, still in tree-shade. "It's a beautiful day," he said, and followed that up with an explanation, of sorts. "I saw you heading down here, so I came along to meet you."

Eleanor's expression tightened noticeably, as it always did when she faced Paul Fleming. She said, "Good morning, Sergeant," and sat her saddle with a closed expression. "Yes, it's a beautiful day."

He said, "I need your help, Mrs Marchant. There isn't any tactful way to say this — to explain why I need your help. I know where you got the money you sent your father. I know about Blassingame's offer, and I *think* I understand his terms, which evidently you rejected because he did not give you the money, and when you told Clarence Dunning about those terms, Lamont Blassingame was killed so that he wouldn't be able to tell your husband — or anyone else, for the matter of that — what Blassingame had discovered."

Fleming paused and studied the smooth face in front of him. The colour had receded but otherwise Eleanor Marchant showed nothing. She did not drop her eyes nor move as though to ride past. Fleming began to wonder if he had made an incorrect appraisal; whether she was a lot more cold-blooded than he had surmised. If she was, then he wasn't going to get any help from her — and short of arresting her to prevent it, he was not going to be able to prevent her from telephoning Dunning, who had already killed one man to keep their secret.

He went on speaking. "There is a lot more. Some of it I'm sure that even you don't know. I can tell you one thing that may help you arrive at a decision: Clarence Dunning is face to face with a charge of first-degree murder."

She still sat up there looking like a pale carving.

Fleming decided to force her, so he said, "Did you know Dunning was going to kill Lamont Blassingame?"

She very slowly shook her head. When she answered, the word was almost a whisper. "No."

"But you told him about meeting Blassingame?"

"Yes."

"Why?" asked Fleming.

In a slightly strong voice she said, "Because I had to. Because Monty said that unless I stopped seeing Clarence at once he was going to take a hand."

Fleming was interested. "What did he mean, take a hand?"

"He was going to put a stop to it himself. He told me that right after I said I wouldn't accept his money on his terms. He said that unless I stopped seeing Clarence immediately, he would see to it that I never had the opportunity to see him again."

Fleming pondered that. It sounded like a threat to him. "Did Blassingame mean he would tell your husband or your father-in-law?"

Eleanor moved her head very gently from side to side. "No. If he'd said that — I know

now that Clarence would only have laughed. He didn't care what happened to me; in fact, I think he *wanted* my husband to know. He is intensely jealous of the Marchant name and wealth."

"What *did* Blassingame mean, then?" Fleming asked.

"He said he would break Clarence. He said if it cost him five million dollars he would buy enough shares in every company Clarence was involved with, and he would then systematically destroy Clarence, financially."

Fleming blew out a long breath. So *that* was why Dunning had killed Blassingame. Not to keep his affair with beautiful Eleanor Marchant secret, but to protect his *fortune*. Blassingame may have been gallant, at least in the sense that he did not want to hurt old Peter or his son, or even Eleanor, actually, but he had also been very careless. A man who had climbed to a position of wealth the way Dunning had, would be devoid of ethics; in a cornered position, he would be very dangerous. Blassingame, the honest, rough old widower with a soft spot in his heart for a girl who reminded him of a woman he had loved very much, because he *did* have ethics, overlooked the one thing that really mattered, and that, simply, was that when he threatened Dunning through Eleanor Marchant, he had left Dunning no real alternative except to shut Blassingame up for ever.

"Did he tell you that he would kill Lamont Blassingame?" asked Fleming, and saw the lovely eyes darken with pain.

"No. He only told me not to come near him again. He said I was a fool and a — whore — and that now my husband, the very proper and powerful Richard Marchant, could have back his damaged goods. He did not say anything at all about Monty. He just told me never to come near him again."

Fleming saw his case against Dunning slipping away in fragments. "How many times did you visit him at his house, Mrs Marchant?"

". . . Three times. Otherwise — I'd drive into the city to go shopping, and we'd meet." She looked at the horse's neck, placed a gentle hand upon its mane, weaving the fingers through the hair.

"When you were in his house, Mrs Marchant, did you see a rifle?"

She nodded, still with her eyes averted. "Yes. Several rifles, in fact. He had them in a gun cabinet in his study."

"Would you recognise them if you saw them again?" asked Fleming, and held his breath.

She said, "No, I don't think I would. One gun looks like every other gun to me, Sergeant."

He thought a moment, and in this interim of silence she raised her face a little and looked at him. "Am I under arrest?" she asked, dropping her voice so low he almost did not hear her.

Fleming did not answer except to shake his head. He was cursing himself for not bringing along the radio transceiver. He remembered the white-coated servant who had brought Dunning that iced highball on the verandah the only time Fleming had ever spoken to Dunning. The servant, a man, would remember a gun, more than likely. Sublette would be somewhere up there, by the Dunning residence; if he knew what Fleming now knew, Sublette could interrogate the servant before Clarence Dunning had any inkling about what was happening.

Eleanor Marchant's horse got impatient. She controlled it with a slight movement of the reins and a quiet word. Fleming looked up at her again. "I'm going to ask you not to ride home now and telephone Clarence Dunning. You're evidently not implicated in the murder, Mrs Marchant, but the minute you help Dunning from this moment on, you are going to be involved. And in case you don't really believe Dunning is now your enemy, I can tell you for a fact that although he gave you that two hundred thousand dollars with no strings attached — at least, no *written* terms — a little later he started buying up Davis-Whiting shares, and except for someone else who also started buying them up, Dunning would by now have your father in his pocket." Fleming looked past, across the bridle path in the general direction of the distant glade where a number of birds were making a racket in the treetops. Then he drifted his glance back to the beautiful woman. "Go on, now, and finish your ride." Fleming stepped aside as Eleanor Marchant heeled her horse onward. As she passed he could see the strange, hot dryness of her eyes and the loose and shattered expression down around her mouth.

CHAPTER 19

THE BEGINNING
OF THE END

Fleming waited patiently. As a youngster he had seen birds in treetops act like that any number of times, and, of course, if he had wished to move out into the open a short distance, he could also see the elder Marchant's cottage up there upon the rolling lip of the north-easterly hillock.

He lit a cigarette, gazed briefly down where Eleanor was passing on around the curve, and when she could no longer see him back there, Fleming strode to the far side of the path and said, "Come on out. She's gone."

Peter Marchant stepped silently into view. He was carrying a hiking staff. Until he came out of the gloom so that Fleming could see his face, it was impossible to guess how much he had heard. Then, as he shuffled closer, it was easier for Fleming to make his judgement from the way the older man walked, than by how he looked.

Fleming leaned on the fence. "You heard it all?"

Peter Marchant halted, leaned on his staff and gazed in the direction his daughter-in-law had disappeared. "I heard it all," he said.

"Then you'll know it was Dunning, not Blassingame, she was seeing."

"Yes." Marchant looked over at Fleming. "Dunning all the way. I don't know what to say."

Fleming had no idea, either, but he thought he knew what old Marchant might *do*. "If she telephones Dunning when she reaches the stables, someone else could get hurt. I suppose, if a man were a good hiker, he could cut up the slope and reach the stable before she got there, riding slow and having more territory to cover."

Marchant stood listening, and looking at Fleming. For a long moment he did not move. It was Fleming's impression that he was still in shock. Then someone sang out from a short distance, making Fleming look around. It was Mike Sublette coming in a thrusting walk down across the open, grassy slope from the direction of the Dunning residence. When Fleming glanced back, the elder Marchant was gone up through the glade towards the sidehill.

Sublette came up looking hot and a little winded. In an annoyed voice he said, "Where the hell is your radio? I've been calling you for twenty minutes."

Fleming avoided the question by asking one of his own. "Why? What's happening?"

"I can't locate Dunning. His houseboy said he left early this morning. He thinks he may have gone visiting at one of the other estates, but he doesn't know. Dunning doesn't tell the guy where he goes, he just drives off."

Fleming smiled. "Good."

Sublette scowled. "Good? What's good about it? You said you wanted to know where he was and to keep tabs on him."

Fleming turned. "Come along. I'd rather talk to the houseboy. My car's down here about a half-mile."

Sublette vaulted the fence and fell in beside Fleming. He had recovered from his recent downhill hike, but he was still limp from heat and exertion. "Why the houseboy?" he asked, swinging along.

"Because Eleanor Marchant said there's a gun-rack in the study, and I'm praying very hard one gun will be missing and that the houseboy'll remember which gun."

When they got to the car and Fleming was backing clear to whirl and drive back around towards the southerly entrance to Forest Hills, Mike opened the jockey-box, saw the transceiver lying there, closed the jockey-box and swore with feeling. But he did not make an issue of it; he'd had to hike down that exposed rolling slope of pasture for something like a half-mile under a broiling sun because he had been unable to raise Fleming on the two-way, but it was done, so to hell with it. Next time, though . . .

As they turned in the south entranceway Fleming related the results of his interview with Mrs Marchant, and afterwards with her father-in-law. Sublette was of the opinion that it might be a good idea if one of them went along to the Marchant place and re-mained there at least until Dunning was located.

Fleming was not too concerned. He had faith in old Peter Marchant.

As they climbed out of the car in front of the Dunning residence, the houseboy ap-peared in the doorway, smiling broadly, al-though it was hardly to be expected that he was pleased to see a pair of burly detectives drive up. *No* one, even people with nothing to fear, enjoyed seeing detectives in their driveway.

Fleming went over to the wide patio, nod-ded pleasantly and asked the houseboy if he had any idea where Mister Dunning was. As the servant replied that he had no idea, he shot Mike a quizzical look, as though to imply that Mike should have told Sergeant Fleming. Mike ignored the look.

Fleming said, "Do you suppose we could go inside?" He had no warrant. The house-boy reacted according to his training by moving far back into the entry-hall and motioning for the visitors to enter. They did, but when Fleming asked if they might see the study, the houseboy's expression lost some of its spontaneous geniality. He hesitated, so Mice Sublette smilingly told him they would only look in for a moment, and that seemed to have some influence, because the houseboy led the way.

Clarence Dunning's long, rambling, country-style residence was as beautifully furnished as Fleming had never for a moment doubted but that it would be. The study was partly vertical redwood and partly some kind of monk's cloth, or tightly but roughly woven dark burlap. It sounded terrible, but as a matter of fact the combination between red wood and burlap was quite pleasantly striking.

The gun cabinet was built into the north wall to the right of the fieldstone fireplace. There were two shotguns, two rifles, and three pistols behind the break-front glass doors. There was also a place for another gun between the pair of rifles.

Fleming turned to the houseboy, who looked to be either an Indonesian or a Philippino. He was greying and except for that he could have been no more than perhaps thirty or thirty-five years of age. More likely he was about fifty, perhaps even a little older.

"A rifle is missing," said Fleming and watched the pleasant, quick, bright dark eyes jump to the gun cabinet. "Old gun," said the houseboy. "No good anyway." He raised a smiling countenance to Fleming. "I know that kind of old gun. When I was young I had one. That was on Mindanao after the Japanese came." The smiling face seemed to sharpen slightly under the force of recollection. "They were old guns even that far back. Shoot good, but too slow."

Fleming nodded his sympathetic understanding. "When was the last time you saw that particular old gun?"

The houseboy pondered. "Maybe three weeks ago. I don't remember exactly. Maybe a month ago."

"More than a month?" asked Fleming, and the houseboy vigorously shook his head.

"No. No more than a month ago. I dusted in here; dusted inside all the bookcases. Also dusted inside gun cabinet. Old gun was there then. I remember, because I take the guns out to dust, then put them back. That old gun had screw-threads on the end of the barrel, very unusual thing. The sight was gone and it have maybe three screw-threads up there."

Fleming said, "What calibre gun was it?"

The houseboy answered immediately. "Old thirty-ought-six."

"Would you recognise that particular old

gun if you ever saw it again?" asked Mike Sublette, and as the houseboy faced Mike he smiled broadly again.

"Yes. I never saw one with screw-threads on the barrel like that before. Also, there was particular scratches on wood. Like I said, I know that kind of old gun. When I dust in here, and hold it, I remember a lot of things. You see?"

Fleming 'saw'. He led the way back towards the front of the house, and as they reached the entry way the telephone rang. The houseboy turned, but Sublette was quicker. With a smile Mike said, "If that is Mister Dunning, don't tell him we are here." Mike then lifted the telephone and handed it to the houseboy.

The conversation was brisk and almost exclusively one-sided, and as the houseboy afterwards replaced the telephone he looked a little quizzically at Mike Sublette. "That was Mister Dunning. He is going to stay down at the golf club for the rest of the afternoon, then have dinner there. He say I don't have to make dinner . . . Say, I'm beginning to wonder about something . . . You want a lot of information about that old gun. Mister Blassingame was shot maybe two weeks ago." He did not come right out and ask, but his eyes went slowly from Mike to Fleming, then back again to Sublette. When neither detective said anything, the houseboy leaned against the entry wall and looked down at the telephone. "You think Mister Dunning did that, don't you?" he asked softly, bringing his head up and gazing closely at Sublette again. "You think Mister Dunning use that old gun to kill Mister Blassingame, don't you?"

Mike left whatever had to be said up to Paul Fleming. This was Fleming's case. But the houseboy, perhaps because Sublette had been around longer today, had fixed upon Mike as his acquaintance, so when Fleming finally spoke, the houseboy turned towards him only reluctantly.

"We think *someone* used that old gun to kill Mister Blassingame, yes. And now we need you as a witness about the old gun. Can you testify in court and say exactly what you've told us this afternoon?"

The houseboy's muddy eyes dropped. After a while he said, "I can do that, yes." He looked at Mike again. "Mister Dunning did *that?*"

Sublette lifted thick shoulders and dropped them, still silent.

Fleming was also silent, but for a different reason. He was debating whether to have Mike take the houseboy into the city, or whether to leave him here and have Mike stay with him until Dunning could be collared at the golf club. It would be relatively simple to have the prosecuting attorney's office serve the houseboy with a subpoena as a material witness, but first Fleming had to present a workable case to the prosecuting attorney, and these things took time. If the houseboy suddenly had a change of heart, perhaps with financial inducement from Dunning, Fleming's case would go down the drain. Actually, except for the old gun, he only had the houseboy's testimony to tie Dunning to the murder weapon. Without the houseboy's testimony in court, all Fleming had was an old gun, a dead man, and some valid — but unsubstantiated — suspicions.

Sublette was perhaps thinking along these same lines because he broke the silence by saying, "Go on up to the golf club and nail him. I'll stay here. By the way, you *did* bring that John Doe warrant with you, didn't you?"

Fleming patted his jacket. The warrant was inside. He gazed at the houseboy a moment, then nodded his head. "Okay, I'll call for a prowl car after I make the arrest, then I'll come back here." He smiled at the houseboy. "You've been a big help. We appreciate that very much."

The Philippino did not look very happy. "But I never thought it would be Mister Blassingame," he muttered. "I thought someone might get hurt, but maybe the lady's husband or Mister Dunning. But I never even thought Mister Blassingame . . . Why him? Mister Dunning didn't even go over there, maybe once or twice a year."

Fleming winked at Mike. "Good luck," he said, and let himself out of the house where shadows were beginning to form along the east side of the building. It seemed a little cooler, because of those shadows, but actually it was still a very warm day.

Fleming started on around the far side of Dunning's horse-shoe-shaped private drive towards the yonder main thoroughfare, and did not see the large, dark car moving slowly as though to intercept him until he was almost to the entrance, then he saw it come to a slow halt blocking his exit.

Richard Marchant, attired in a sport shirt open at the neck and a light cashmere jacket, got out and stood beside the car watching Fleming come to a halt.

Fleming alighted, made his appraisal of the larger and younger man, and walked ahead without taking his eyes off Marchant. When he was close he said, "Did you want to see me?"

Marchant looked stonily at Fleming. "I finished talking to my wife a few minutes ago, Sergeant, and saw your car up there." The haggard face tilted upwards in the direction of Dunning's hilltop residence. "Where is he?"

Fleming thought he understood and said,

"Go on home, Mister Marchant."

"Not just yet. Tell me where Dunning is."

Fleming considered. He had absolutely no intention of allowing young Marchant to add to his woes by doing something rash; on the other hand, he could not take the time right now to argue. He finally said, "Get in my car. I'll take you back up there." As Marchant walked towards him Fleming sighed to himself. Mike wasn't going to like being saddled with young Marchant, but he could handle this fresh situation a lot better than Fleming could. The main thing was to prevent more trouble. The next most important thing was to find Clarence Dunning and put him under arrest. After that, it would be anyone's guess how the thing would be concluded.

CHAPTER 20

A NEAR THING

The golf club was evidently in the process of being enlivened by some kind of nightly entertainment when Fleming drove into the parking area. He could hear music, there were a number of people, mostly couples, strolling the bland shade of the late afternoon out front and even in the direction of the parking area, and it seemed that every light in the low, long building had been switched on.

He left the car and moved through the warm gloom where a windbreak of immense eucalyptus trees formed a backdrop behind the clubhouse. The greens stretched away on both sides and out front of the place, lending an appearance of spaciousness.

A young man with long pale hair came past carrying an empty tray and Fleming intercepted him to ask what the occasion was. "Tournament starts tomorrow," said the waiter. "Every year they have a pre-tournament dinner-dance." The young man's expression turned sardonic. "Big deal," he said, and walked on towards a rear doorway. Fleming understood the young man's sentiment without necessarily sympathising with it. Big deal; all the wealthy *entrepreneurs* of rich and exclusive Forest Hills gathered this evening to celebrate their annual golfing *fête*, and everywhere else people were struggling hard just to cope with skyrocketing inflation and a world becoming increasingly ominous. The trouble with being as idealistic and 'committed' as that young man obviously felt himself to be was that it changed nothing, and therefore one human being could do a lot worse than live his life as though decent things mattered.

Fleming moved off in the direction of the front verandah; he had an idea that without making himself conspicuous he would probably encounter Clarence Dunning around there, sooner or later. He had no intention of bursting in full of authority and making a scene of the apprehension, especially since he was sure Dunning suspected nothing.

Out front, women in cocktail dresses and a few men — not very many — in white evening jackets mingled with people dressed in more or less casual, everyday attire. It was evidently one of those affairs among the

207

very wealthy that was not *de rigeur,* and that seemed to Fleming in keeping with the approach to life very wealthy people could afford to have; they did not have to impress other people and could therefore be themselves. It was a good way to be, if a person could manage it.

Another young man bearing a tray, this one with several frosted glasses on it, came by with a smile. Fleming declined the offer, also with a smile, and lit a cigarette as he settled back against the front wall in the shadows.

People-watching was interesting at almost any time and Fleming was an inveterate at it. He saw a very lovely girl who was perhaps no more than nineteen or twenty stroll past on the arm of a greying, athletic man old enough to be her father. He also saw a rather sharp-featured older man, built like a wrestler, go stand wide-legged at the edge of the patio, scowling out across the park-like greens. Fleming smiled to himself; Napoleon probably had looked very much like that — without the martini glass in his hand — when he'd glowered across the Channel towards unconquerable Britain.

Fleming did not recognise any of these people. Evidently they were all from within the private Forest Hills domain, since the club was that exclusive, and while he knew that Forest Hills encompassed several miles of countryside, it still seemed that there were an awful lot of people at the club this evening. Probably some were guests; that, at least, would be permissible.

He decided Dunning would not appear outside, after all, and strolled towards an open french door. The musicians were evidently in another, more distant large room for although their music was louder the moment Fleming entered the main lounge, he could not see them.

There were people sitting or standing, all across the main lounge, which was a very handsome room. Off to one side, through an archway, beyond an antique wrought-iron screen, was the bar. It seemed to have twice as many people as the lounge held. A curly-headed man came up and gave Fleming a worried look. It was the club manager. Fleming thought his expression probably sprang from some apprehension Fleming's appearance at the club might have aroused, but the manager leaned and said, "I have a message for you, Sergeant Fleming. I've been looking all over for you. The man who called said under no circumstances for me to have you paged."

Fleming said, "What man?" and got an immediate response.

"Mike Sublette. Does that convey anything to you?"

"It does. What's the message?"

"That Mrs Marchant is on her way to the club."

Fleming stared at the curly-headed man a moment. If Eleanor Marchant was on her way, that meant that she had called the Dunning residence. Otherwise Mike probably would not have known she was coming. If she had called Dunning's house it was to talk to Dunning — to warn him, perhaps, but another possibility also crossed Fleming's mind. He nodded to the manager and said, "Thanks," then he stepped back out to the verandah and walked quickly to the south end of the building where he had a good view of the distant roadway. When he saw the car lights coming slowly, he stamped out his cigarette and stepped off the verandah.

By the time Fleming reached the parking area there were three additional sets of headlamps approaching, but these were coming from the north. That other car had come from the south. Fleming went out through the cars until he could make out the oncoming vehicle well enough, then he waited until it pulled smoothly into a vacant space, and when Eleanor Marchant alighted — still in her riding clothes — Fleming stepped up beside her.

She whirled, gripping a large leather purse as though to protect it. When she recognised Fleming she acted slightly breathless, slightly confused. Fleming's hunch was strong now. He held out his left hand for the purse. Neither of them said anything. Eleanor Marchant shot a quick glance over one shoulder, as though she wanted to flee. There was a car back there, facing her. She was blocked behind and in front.

Fleming reached and gently took the purse, opened it, saw the shiny black gun, lifted it out and handed back the purse. He eased back the slide so that fading daylight glinted evilly off a brass cartridge casing. When he eased the slide forward and set the safety-catch, he raised his head. Eleanor Marchant was standing unsteadily with one hand outstretched to support herself against the car.

Fleming said, "What good would that do?"

She shook her head in a ragged motion and kept silent.

Fleming reached for her arm and led her along with him over to where his car was parked, and while still holding her he reached inside for his radio speaker. It only took a moment to call for a prowl car. Afterwards, he released her arm and felt pity. There really was nothing to say; pointing out to someone who was irrational with shock and self-loathing that shooting the person responsible for their predicament would only make matters worse, was useless and

Fleming knew it. He had been here before, many times.

Maybe, after the shock had worn off, Eleanor Marchant would understand how close she had come to ruining her life, *really* ruining it. But that was her problem, not Fleming's; detectives were not priests nor were they authorised to act like priests.

She finally let out a rattling sigh and seemed to gain some measure of self-control. Her beautiful face lifted, the eyes seeking Fleming's eyes. "What happens to me now?" she murmured.

Fleming had two choices. He chose the lesser of two evils. "You're going to be taken back home and kept there. Otherwise, you can be taken in and jailed on a charge of carrying a concealed weapon, which isn't much of a charge any more, but at least it'll keep you away from Dunning until I can pick him up. I'd rather not book you; you'd be released in the morning, but the newspapers would have a field-day about it. Mrs Marchant, leave it up to the law."

She kept staring at Fleming. "Sergeant, the law doesn't work against rich people."

He could have agreed with her on that, in most cases, but he also knew something she apparently did not know: that judges and especially juries were very hard on rich people who committed murder. Anyone of power who tried to act above the law was far more liable to be unrelentingly prosecuted than someone of a lesser social position. All he told her was: "If you will help the law, believe me, Clarence Dunning's wealth won't buy him anything except some good lawyers. Shooting him would only put you up there right beside his kind. If you really want to repay him, be a witness for the prosecution."

He saw her face tighten with that expression she usually used towards him, and thought he understood. As a car wheeled in from the north with a revolving red light atop it, Fleming said, "Of course there'll be publicity, if that's what worrying you, Mrs Marchant. There's no way I know of to prevent that. Maybe that's part of the price people pay for being able to live in places like Forest Hills. I'm sorry." He motioned towards the police cruiser. "Let's go."

Both the big uniformed officers were alighting from their vehicle when Fleming took Eleanor Marchant out to them. He identified himself, asked the officers to take her to her residence, and asked that they remain with her for a half-hour or so, until Fleming could call in that he had arrested the man he was looking for at the country club. He did not hand over the pistol he had taken from her, did not even mention it. The uniformed men gazed dispassionately at Eleanor, then one stepped back and opened the rear door of their car. This same officer nodded at Fleming, who turned and strolled back towards the lighted clubhouse. Nothing over there seemed changed at all, people were still talking, laughing, strolling the warm late evening, and the music was as pleasant and as subdued as ever, but Fleming had scarcely stepped back on to the front patio when the curly-headed manager appeared out of the deepening shadows looking quizzical.

"I hope everything went off properly," he said, and Fleming, without feeling anything for this man one way or the other, but mindful of his cooperation a week back, said that everything was just fine. Then he asked if the curly-headed man had seen Clarence Dunning, and got a nod.

"He was in the bar a short while ago, Sergeant. If you want him I could —"

"No, thanks," Fleming said quickly. "By any chance did you happened to mention to him that I'm here this evening?"

The curly-headed man hadn't. "There is precious little time just for meeting everyone as they arrive, at these gatherings, Sergeant, let alone time enough to sit and have a drink with anyone." The manager's expression slowly underwent a change. He stared at Fleming in about the same way Dunning's houseboy had stared — as though a very gradual, and very shattering, thought had just begun to fill his mind. Fleming knew the look and stepped past.

The curly-headed man turned very slowly to watch. Fleming was unaware of this. It would not have bothered him very much even had he known. As he went back to the glass doors again, entering the lounge for the second time, he paused just inside to light a cigarette, to afterwards scan the room without haste, and when he failed to catch sight of Dunning, he started across towards that antique wrought-iron scrollwork that discreetly masked the arched doorway to the yonder bar-room.

The music was a little louder in the bar-room. The lighting was much more subdued in there, too. Beyond, where another of those rather Moorish arched doorways separated the bar-room from the dance-floor, Fleming finally caught sight of the musicians. They were upon a slightly raised, long platform, and they were immaculate in white dinner jackets.

The bar-room itself was a surprisingly large room. Actually, it was longer than it was wide by perhaps twice the distance. The bar itself was a very handsome mahogany affair with spotless rows of bottles upon equally as spotless glass shelves behind, where there was indirect lighting. The bar-room seemed to have about as many occupants as either the dance-floor or the lounge.

Fleming strolled down the full length of the bar looking at the hip-to-shoulder patrons sitting along there. The smoke was both fragrant and thick. It might have further hindered visibility, along with the subdued lighting, if a soundless and invisible air filtration system was not working hard somewhere.

He also looked among the people seated at the little tables in the bar-room, and still saw no sign of Clarence Dunning. Then he lingered in the far arched doorway gazing on out across the dance-floor — and saw him.

CHAPTER 21

MAKING THE ARREST

There was no denying that Clarence Dunning was a handsome man; Fleming moved into the room beyond the bar watching the dancers and thought 'distinctive' would really be the single best word to describe Dunning. He was interested, too, in the woman Dunning was dancing with. She had a sprinkling of grey over each temple, her hair was swept upwards around each ear, and it glistened. She was a striking woman, perhaps thirty-five or forty. Possibly even slightly past forty, it was difficult to say from that distance and under that kind of lighting. But she was obviously enjoying herself in Dunning's arms.

Fleming moved to a small empty table near the arched doorway and had barely taken a seat when a cocktail waiter appeared. What Fleming would have liked was a glass of beer, but at a place like the Forest Hills golf club people simply did not drink beer. Fleming ordered a martini, and when it came he let it sit there in front of him; it was his excuse for occupying a table, evidently, because no one bothered him after it arrived.

There were several other doors leading out of the dance-floor, but nine-tenths of all traffic passed in and out by way of the bar-room. Fleming was satisfied to wait until Clarence Dunning passed the table heading in that direction, but just in case Dunning might decide to use one of the other exits, Fleming kept a close watch.

Eventually, when the music stopped and there was an intermission, Dunning took the handsome greying woman to a table where two thick and greying older men were in deep discussion, and where another woman sat, looking bored. Dunning flashed a dazzling smile then he turned and started around the edge of the dance-floor in Fleming's direction. Fleming killed his cigarette and eased back his chair, but a short distance away some people at another table called to Dunning. He went over and stood talking and laughing. Fleming decided that the killing of Lamont Blassingame did not prey on Dunning's mind one bit; he doubted very much that Dunning even thought about it now, unless to speculate on how perfectly he had planned it and how well he had brought it off.

Then Dunning bowed very slightly and turned to resume his passage towards Fleming, and the doorway beyond. Fleming let him get almost abreast of the little table before he stood up. That was when Dunning recognised him. The killer's strong, self-assured stride seemed to hesitate, but just for a second or two, then Dunning's genial smile came up and he veered over towards the table with his right hand extended.

"How are you, Sergeant?" he said, shaking Fleming's hand. "You surprised me, being here this evening."

Fleming said, "Did I? Have a seat, Mister Dunning."

"Well, I'd really like to, Sergeant, but I'm supposed to meet some—"

"Have a seat!"

Dunning's smile froze as his eyes met Fleming's stone-steady and unsmiling stare. Without another word Dunning pulled out a chair and sat. Fleming did the same, opposite Dunning. For five seconds neither of them spoke nor looked away. Over Dunning's shoulder Paul Fleming saw the musicians getting into position to start playing again. He thought that would be a good time for he and Dunning to make their discreet exodus; when everyone else was standing up and moving. He said, "Mister Dunning, you are under arrest."

The financier's face did not register the feigned surprise Fleming expected. In fact, it registered nothing at all as Dunning said, "Sergeant, you'd better damned well know what you are doing."

Fleming could see the musicians, they were now ready. He leaned and said, "Suppose we avoid some embarrassment for you and everyone else in here. When I stand up, you do the same. Then you walk right on through the bar-room to the lounge, and out the french doors to the patio. Don't do anything heroic, will you, Mister Dunning?"

The financier eased back in his chair. "Of course I won't do anything heroic. Why should I? What a ridiculous thing you're doing, Sergeant. What specifically am I being arrested for?"

"Murder one. Murder in the first degree, Mister Dunning. Are you ready to leave now?"

Dunning ignored the question and continued to sit there staring across the table. "You can't possibly be serious."

Fleming sighed. "Look, you lied when you said you'd played golf a couple of times with Lamont Blassingame. I've got the club records to prove you lied about that. Then there's something else you did recently — bought that swampy glade down where the bridle path curves. No one else wanted it, but all of a sudden it became important to you. You bought it. Would you like me to tell you why you bought it?"

Dunning's thin, long mouth drew upwards in a death's-head grin. "I bought it for speculation. But if you have some other wild theory, yes, Sergeant, I'd like to hear it."

Fleming said, "I can do better, Dunning. I can show you why you bought that land. It didn't cost much, you could afford the price, and it ensured that no one else would go puttering about trying to develop it. I've got the gun you buried, Mister Dunning, and I've got the positive identification of it as well."

Clarence Dunning's eyes dulled momentarily as a shadow passed across his face. Then he said, "Ridiculous. Are you accusing me of shooting Monty Blassingame?"

Fleming leaned to rise. "Yes, and I think we've got a fair case against you. Now stand up and lead off."

Dunning did not move until Fleming was standing, then he rose too. As he turned he said, "You'd better have a good case, Sergeant, or you're going to find yourself in the damndest counter-suit you ever imagined." He stopped suddenly and turned. "Why would I have killed Blassingame?"

Fleming reached and gave his prisoner a gentle shove. "Keep walking."

They passed through the bar to the lounge, and several times along the way people hailed Dunning. Fleming could not help but

221

admire the murderer's *elan*. He waved and called greetings and smiled with all his customary charm, and kept right on walking. When they had passed through the glass doors to the front verandah, Dunning paused, stepped aside for Fleming to come abreast of him and, as he patted his pockets for a lighter to fire up the cigarette in his mouth, he said, "Match, Sergeant?"

Fleming handed over a packet of lights. This was the time, after the shock, the mental disarray, had been replaced by the sensation of being captured, that criminals did whatever they felt they had to do. Fleming stood waiting; he was even a little anticipatory. He felt no inhibitions about putting Clarence Dunning flat down on his back with one solid punch.

But Dunning handed back the matchbook, said, "Thanks," and turned towards the parking lot. "I suppose we're going in the right direction, aren't we?" he said breezily, and did nothing rash nor desperate.

There was no real reason for him to do anything desperate. A man of Dunning's character was a good judge of humanity. He wouldn't have had to have been to see that Sergeant Fleming was capable of handling any physical reaction Dunning might have considered, but more to the point, Clarence Dunning the millionaire had his wealth to rely on.

When they reached the car and Dunning started to get into the back, Fleming told him to sit up front, and Dunning obeyed. As they were leaving the club Dunning blew out a big gust of smoke, looked over and said, "Do you realise what your chances probably are of bringing this off, Sergeant?"

Fleming gave his stock reply to this question. It was not entirely factual, but it usually shut them up. "Probably about fair, Mister Dunning. That's the prosecuting attorney's job, anyway, not mine." He picked up the radio speaker, called for the uniformed men at the Marchant house, got one of them outside at their prowl car, and gave them an all-clear to return to their beat. He asked to have someone telephone Sublette, down at the Dunning residence, and tell Mike to meet Fleming at the south gateway. Then he replaced the speaker on its dashboard hook and drove without any haste because if he got down to the gateway before Mike arrived he would simply have to sit there and wait — and probably listen to Clarence Dunning, something he really did not much care about doing.

But Dunning, who had heard Fleming's instructions, spoke up as they were cruising southward, so Fleming had to listen to him anyway.

"What's your man doing at my house, Sergeant? I hope you had a warrant for entering the grounds."

Fleming kept his gaze on the road ahead as he answered. "I don't need a warrant to enter your grounds, Mister Dunning. Under California law everyone's front door has to be available to the public, which means the police."

Dunning digested this thoughtfully, then spoke again. "How do you propose to prove I shot Monty Blassingame? Were there witnesses?"

Fleming skirted that one without much difficulty. "How are *you* going to prove that you did *not* shoot him? If I were in your boots that'd worry me a hell of a lot more than anything else."

Dunning flipped out his smoke and glanced towards the Marchant house atop its magnificent hill as they cruised past it. "Sergeant," he said in a perfectly calm, conversational tone of voice, "give me one answer, and I'll stop pestering you with questions." He turned towards Fleming. "Is Eleanor Marchant involved in this case you have been building against me?"

Fleming was reluctant to answer that, but on the other hand Dunning's lawyers would know no later than tomorrow that she was very much involved, so he said, "Yes." Then he saw the red tail-lamps up ahead leaving the Dunning driveway and picked up a little speed so as to arrive down there about the same time Mike reached the entrance.

Dunning said no more, not even when Fleming pulled in behind Sublette and ordered him to get out and go up front to the other car.

Mike glanced almost casually at Dunning and reached under his jacket and brought forth handcuffs. He shrugged at Fleming as though to say he thought it was a silly rule too, but he was not going to disobey it. He strolled over, told Dunning to hold out his hands, cuffed him, then put him into the car, locked the door from the outside, then went back where Fleming was leaning, looking pensively back up towards the lighted Blassingame mansion, and said, "I sent young Marchant home. He's not really the violent type anyway. You got Eleanor, the patrolmen informed me. Did she go up there to warn him?"

Fleming looked back towards Mike. "To shoot him." He dug out the pistol and offered it to Sublette. Mike took the small weapon and looked disgusted. "What the hell would that prove — except that she'd be in grief up to her gullet?"

"It would prove she's a woman," said Fleming. "And in my experience, a badly upset woman is about as likely to employ reason as a horse is. Look, book our boy on suspicion of murder, be sure you inform him of his rights on the way in, and put him to bed. I'm going back up to the Marchant place for a little while."

Sublette nodded. "Okay. Dunning's houseboy's going to be a good witness. If Eleanor will be just half as solid, I think we've got Mister Big right where the hair is short." Sublette winked, then turned and went over to his car, got in and drove out through the entranceway, turned right and headed off towards the city.

Fleming waited. The loose ends he had to tie up weren't pressing, and it was very pleasant just standing there in the early night.

There was no moon, but it was perhaps a little early for it to be coming over the mountains yet. He went slowly and calmly back over the Blassingame case in his mind and did not get back into the car to drive to the Marchant estate until he was satisfied that he had a good chance, a *very* good chance, if Eleanor would testify, of putting a murderer away for life.

He needed reassurance Eleanor would testify. After he got that, he could go home. As he turned up the Marchant drive he yawned, but it wasn't even nine o'clock.

CHAPTER 22

NIGHT FOLLOWS EVENING

They must have been expecting him. At least it looked that way because they were all in the study when the servant escorted Fleming to them.

Peter Marchant looked his age, something Fleming had not especially noticed about him before. His son had all the reason in the world to have that glass in his hand. Fleming had no idea how much liquor he had consumed, but it did not appear to have done him any harm, nor any good either. There were times, as Fleming knew, when taking on a load of the stuff did not help a man escape regardless of the amount he drank.

Eleanor looked small and frail. She avoided Fleming, but the men didn't. Richard offered a chair and asked if Dunning had been arrested.

Fleming ignored the chair because he had

no desire to stay in this house full of recrimination and anguish one moment longer than he had to. In response to young Marchant's enquiry he said, "He was at the golf club. Now he's in custody." Fleming looked at Eleanor, but he was still addressing Richard when he went on speaking. "The hardest part lies ahead. I need depositions and witnesses for the prosecution. I need Mrs Marchant's particular support, and that means a lot of unsavoury publicity. I wish there was a way to do this without the press, but there isn't. If she testifies, it's all going to get into the newspapers."

Eleanor sat looking stonily into the cold fireplace. She seemed withdrawn and although she certainly heard what was being said, she gave no sign of it at all.

Old Peter was studying his hands when he said, "It will get into the newspapers anyway, won't it?" What he meant, of course, was that even if Eleanor did not testify, Dunning's defence would inevitably draw her into court, and that was true so Fleming agreed.

"Yes, it'll be in the newspapers either way. But without her to testify about Dunning's motive, there is a fair possibility that he might get a reduced sentence. Criminal prosecution has to prove two things: the commission of a crime and the deliberate intention of committing it. Mrs Marchant can supply both."

Richard drained his glass and went to sit at his desk. He slumped back in the chair gazing over at Fleming in the doorway. "The wages of sin, eh?" he exclaimed softly. "The law of retribution, Sergeant. You've probably seen more of this than any of us, so tell me: does the mud ever come off?"

Fleming leaned in the doorway wishing he was almost anywhere but where he was. "I'm a policeman, Mister Marchant, not a social pundit. All I can tell you is that if Mrs Marchant will help the prosecution, the man who has wiped out one life and who has tried to ruin another life — perhaps more than one life — will learn that there really *is* a law of retribution."

Eleanor still had not looked at Fleming. She did not look at him now as she said, "I'll testify, Sergeant. Is there another choice?"

There really wasn't; she would be subpoenaed by the office of the prosecuting attorney and put on the witness stand under oath. But it always came out much better if witnesses were volunteers, so Fleming said, "No, there isn't much actual choice, Mrs Marchant, but the law needs your help more than it needs your reluctance."

"I said I'd testify, Sergeant," said the woman. "I never wanted *less* to do anything in my entire life. But I'll tell everything exactly as it happened. It that good enough?"

Fleming straightened up. There had to be

something kind he could say, but whatever it was escaped him at the moment. He could tell, too, that she wished he would leave, and he thought he could also understand that; it was terrible enough, being in the same room with her husband at this time, not to mention her father-in-law, but the presence of a person she scarcely knew, but who shared the full knowledge of her degradation, was worse.

He said, "Well, someone from the prosecuting attorney's office will be along in a day or two for talks with all of you." He paused as Peter Marchant got heavily up to his feet. Richard and his wife did not move, did not look at one another, did not in fact seem aware that as Fleming turned to go old Peter shuffled after him.

Fleming said, "Good night," and controlled an urge to hasten to the front door and get beyond it out into the night.

Peter Marchant followed along saying nothing until they were outside. He went down to the car with Fleming, hands thrust deeply into trouser pockets, and when Fleming expected something rambling, disjointed and perhaps even slightly incoherent, old Marchant looked up at him and in a tone of voice that blended with the soft night said, "If you live long enough, Sergeant, you're going to see something like this happen again and again. People are weak, women are weakest. If a man can manage to do nothing after it happens for a year or two, he begins to get a degree of understanding. Not tolerance and not compassion. Understanding. After that, if he keeps his thoughts healthy, he comes back from the shock and the pain. I know."

Fleming thought of the picture of the white-headed woman atop the stereo set in old Marchant's cottage as he stood by the car in the warm, pleasant night, and decided that he liked old Peter Marchant a little more every time he was around him. But there were definite rules about getting involved in conversations with people about things of this nature, in the line of duty. Fleming, the good cop, was also an aware human being. He said, "What's the answer for them, right now?" and old Marchant gave him a quiet answer.

"Let them suffer the torments of the damned with it for a while. I'll know when it's time to intrude, Sergeant. Then of course they'll have to move, have to find another place to live, and that ought to fill a lot of days for them. And a trip after they get re-settled, a sort of re-finding themselves and each other. Richard's got to build more of his life around her; busy, vital women don't have much time for those extra-curricular things, Sergeant. And she's going to have to do the same thing — create her world around him, and around her home, and kids. They've got to produce some kids. Then there's one other thing."

Fleming knew what that was even before old Marchant said it. "Her father?"

The old man smiled slightly. "Her father indeed. And that's where I come in. If I had been a smart man I'd have seen the necessity for this long ago, but hell, I'm just an old has-been. Anyway, I'll pick up those shares Dunning bought and that should give me controlling interest. I'll keep that damned fool out of trouble, down there in Richmond, and it won't really take much of my time. The main thing is, I'll prevent her father from being a worry to her."

Fleming grinned and held out his hand. "Good luck, Mister Marchant." They shook, Fleming got into the car and drove off down the winding roadway. Where he paused to look both ways before turning southward on the main thoroughfare, he glanced back, but it was too dark and the distance was too great; if the old man was still standing out there Fleming did not see him.

He turned right and without conscious effort glanced up where the Blassingame mansion stood. There was a moon now, where there hadn't been before Fleming entered the Marchant house, and its pale light outlined the hilltop residence. Also, there were lights on up there.

Fleming slowed near the private drive and without looking at his watch thought it was still early enough, so he turned up the slope. He was still no more than two-thirds of the way when an amber light added to the brilliance by suddenly illuminating the entry area. Fleming smiled. As with every other residence he had visited in Forest Hills the past couple of weeks, there was no way to approach the Blassingame home, particularly at night when headlamps glared up the hill well in advance of the car, without being seen, providing anyone up there was watching.

He saw someone leave by the front door as he made the final lift and curve that carried his car in a gentle glide the last hundred yards. She kept back on the flagstones until his car stopped and until he climbed out, then she came towards him with a broad smile.

"I thought you might," she said, and did not finish it. She looked up into his face with moonlight and starshine softening each curve and contour. "Well . . . ?"

"Finished," he told her. "Wrapped it up tonight. My partner took Dunning to the city to be booked and locked up." He flapped his arms to indicate both finality and relief. "Damned sordid mess."

She did not press him for details. Instead, she took his arm and paced along around the car towards the south end of the house where the grass underfoot was spongy and pleasant to walk upon. She said, "I should imagine doing something like this month in and month out would eventually — well — almost destroy something in a man."

It was a good thought. "Unless you concentrate on your perspective," he said, "it will. I've known a lot of men who were so sour by the time they retired they didn't even actually like themselves very much."

She looked up at him. "How do you handle it, Paul?"

"By keeping things in perspective; by making a point of looking for two pleasing things for each sordid one." He grinned in the moonlight. "After tonight — after my partner took Dunning away, for example, I went back there and talked to the Marchants. That was pretty damned grim and gloomy. Then old Peter Marchant and I went out by the car and talked a little, and he was the first good thing after the bad thing. Then I drove down here. You're the second good thing." His eyes twinkled in the shadows. "You see? Half an hour ago I couldn't have smiled if my life had depended upon it. But now I can."

She was still clinging to his arm. As they moved slowly towards the rear grounds she leaned closer to him. It did not have to mean anything except that they were friends and that she was fond of him in that way, but of course it did in fact mean more.

"Tomorrow you start a fresh assignment?" she asked, steering him towards the far steps to the raised verandah.

Maybe it would not be tomorrow, but soon he would be given a new assignment. "Not that soon. There is a lot of paperwork connected with homicide investigations. Mike and I still have to wrap up the evidence, the witnesses, the loose ends, and hand them over to the prosecuting attorney." He smiled down at her. "Maybe Sherlock Holmes didn't have to worry about the evidence and the legalities, but I have to. Why, what's on your mind?"

She halted where the stone railing of the verandah was at her back and looked out over the pale-limned warm countryside with its near and distant hilltop lights. "I was thinking how pleasant it could be, Paul, if you could have a holiday." She looked him squarely in the eye. If her cheeks coloured he could not tell, but he did not believe this happened because her lovely dark eyes never wavered even though she had to know that he was putting his own, masculine, interpretation on what she had said.

As a matter of fact he *did* have time off coming. He'd had it coming prior to his assignment to the Blassingame case. Altogether, he had four weeks coming, but it was customary in the bureau for each man to take two weeks in the early summer and the remaining two weeks in the early autumn. He wondered what an entire month with her would be like. If he insisted, Captain McLeod would probably allow it. But that worked a slight hardship on the department.

He said, "If we had two weeks, what would you want to do with it?"

She raised a hand and loosened his tie, reached past with cool fingers and also loosened his collar. "It would be *your* two weeks, Paul. What would *you* want to do with it?"

He had not thought much about his forthcoming holiday lately. Had not, in fact, thought much about it even before being assigned to the Blassingame case. It was something of a department joke about how Paul Fleming along with three or four other bachelor detectives never seemed quite as anxious to get away from the city as everyone else was.

But he did not have much trouble now arriving at a spur-of-the-moment decision. "I would like to spend it," he told Elisabeth Maitland, "lying on an uninhabited beach in Bermuda, with you, watching the surf foam, watching the gulls soar, watching clouds sail by as though there were nothing else in the world."

She reached under his jacket with both arms and pulled herself up close to him with her face turned sideways against his chest. "When do we leave?"

He hadn't looked it up in the holiday roster, so he had no idea, but he said, "How about next Monday? I'll make flight arrangements and call ahead for hotel accommodation."

She snuggled still closer. "I'll go into the city and do my shopping tomorrow. Paul . . . ?"

He lifted her face with a gentle fist. "Yes?"

Her dark eyes were lustrous in a placid way. "It was worth that ten-year wait." She smiled. "I wanted you to know that."

He lowered his head to seek her lips, and she clung to him with surprising strength. Around them, Forest Hills went right on being exactly as it had always been, prior to Fleming's official arrival, and even that hadn't actually changed things very much, only temporarily. Dunning was gone, the tranquillity had returned, and perhaps the mark of distinction that certified that Forest Hills was now an established, traditionalised community was the fact that it had a genuine scandal to discuss in the years ahead.